HAMMER

HAMMER

SAINTS OF CHAOS
BOOK 3

CAYCE POPONEA

EDITED BY
ELIZABETH SIMONTON

GRAPHIC DESIGNER
JADA D'LEE

FOREWORD

A man caught between duty and honor.
    A woman on the cusp of a bright future.
    An instant attraction twisting into love.

Hammer Sheppard is stuck in a toxic relationship, torn between being a good father and doing his job as SOC Vice President. When a medical emergency forces him to hire a new receptionist, will Hammer be able to keep his desires to himself? Or will the timid girl who answered the ad be too tempting to resist?

Emma Shaw has struggled her entire life. She's paid her dues, earning an education and now has a promising career on the horizon. There's only one problem; she needs a temporary job to keep her afloat. What happens when an ad for a receptionist forces her to face the skeletons in her closet? Will Emma keep it professional, or will the allure of the ultimate bad boy be too much to resist?

Emma

CHAPTER
ONE

EMMA

PLEASE LET *me land this job*, I silently prayed, my foot bouncing in rhythm with my racing heart. I needed this position in the worst way, and the advertised salary would carry me until the credentialing process for my dream job was completed.

"Betty Sue Johnson?"

Drifting my gaze to the voice's owner, I spied a slender man dressed in all black, wearing a leather vest decorated with various patches.

"Hey, Keys."

The woman who'd been sitting to my right, jumped to her feet. My gaze drifted from the young man to the lace tops of her thigh-high stockings, which ended two inches before meeting her impossibly short skirt. She walked with ease, despite the height of her heels, placing a kiss to the lips of the man.

"Lavender?" The man questioned, glancing down at the sheet in his hand and then back at the woman.

"Awe, you remembered."

Lavender left no room for question on how the pair knew one another. I watched as confusion morphed into a knowing smile as Keys escorted her down the hall. When they disappeared behind a closed door, I leaned my head back, allowing my mind to drift back to a time when I felt less out of place.

Ten days ago, I'd walked across the stage at graduation, shifting my tassel from one side to the other as I shook the Dean's hand and accepted my diploma.

Having grown up in a single parent home, I'd felt the sting of poverty, deciding at an early age I wanted nothing to do with it as an adult. Using every avenue at my disposal, I paid attention in school and worked every summer. I applied for over three-hundred scholarships, using my high GPA, and community service as my competing edge to move past the other applicants. My hard work paid off, and I was able to attend school tuition free and with enough stipend left over to pay my rent for the next year.

Sadly, there had been no money left for utilities or food. Asking for money from my mother was less than appealing, so I'd begun my job search immediately. My efforts were halted when I woke up two days ago with a severe pain in my left ear. A Google search provided me with the address of a free clinic and while I waited for an antibiotic prescription, I noticed a flier advertising a position for a receptionist and book-keeper for this company.

Laughter from my left pulled me back to the present, and the conversations of the women around me. I envied the way they appeared to know one another, sharing stories of their days and the triumphs and tragedies in their world. Never one to make friends easily, my circle is small and distant, limited to my hair-brained older sister, and a few classmates I kept in touch with from high school

At a time when most teens spread their proverbial wings, indulging in various fraternity parties and other school activities, tasting the freedom of no parental supervision, I was seasoned in what happened when the rum was too strong and inhibitions are weakened, leaving a young person with consequences of their inebriated actions. I'd spent the majority of my college years between the pages of a textbook, the memory of changing my nephew's diaper a sharp reminder to keep my focus.

"Emma Shaw?"

My breath hitched as my name filled the air. An uncomfortable silence blanketed the room as I stood from the plastic chair I'd claimed when I walked in. The click of my heels echoed in the room, the feel of my skirt swishing against my calves, a reminder of how different I was compared to the others waiting their turns. I tried hard not to judge them and their choice in attire; their cut-off shorts, gallons of makeup and acrylic nails, with vibrant colors of hot pink and orange, versus my dark blue suit and kitten heels.

Clutching my messenger bag, a graduation gift from my boyfriend, I covertly released a pent up breath, donning what I hoped was a friendly smile as I closed the distance between myself and Keys.

"I'm Emma Shaw." Extending my hand out to him.

Keys shifted his gaze from my hand to my face, the same knowing smile from before appearing on his lips.

"You ready, darlin'?"

His term of endearment caught me by surprise. I'd been called various degrees of Miss, but never something so…intimate.

"Yes, I believe I am." My voice sounded more confident than I felt.

"Then follow me, beautiful," Keys instructed, adding a wink which made my smile genuine.

With his stature much taller than mine, his long legs pushing him a few feet ahead of me, afforded me an unobstructed view of the back of his vest.

Saints of Chaos was scripted in white on the black top rocker. In preparation for my interview, I'd researched SOC towing, uncovering it was one of many businesses owned by the motorcycle Club. While I was no stranger to the mechanics of one-percent bikers, I wasn't about to get involved in anything outside the parameters of the job they'd hopefully pay me to do. I'd learned from my mother what it was to struggle when the man she placed all her faith in loved the benefits of the Club more than he did the promises he'd made to her.

Hammer

CHAPTER
TWO
HAMMER

FRUSTRATION FILLED my chest as I sat behind the long table, the ringing cell phone in my pocket adding to the cluster fuck of my life. Kira had long since grown tired of being locked away from what she coined a 'normal' life. With the bumps and bruises gone from her body, she'd begun constantly lighting up my phone, threatening to involve the cops if I didn't come and get her.

"Kira again?"

Warden tipped his head toward my Cut, his bent brows mirroring my irritation.

"More than likely," I deadpanned, removing the offending piece of plastic and sending Kira's call to voicemail. I missed the fuck out of my son. His mother, not so much.

"Send in the next one, Keys."

When Doc Ash put Syn on bed rest, we'd put out the call for a temporary receptionist. Raiden gave Erin a flier, which she'd hung in the clinic. Warden and I had agreed, we didn't want another hang around doing the job, yet the lobby was full of them.

Adjusting in my seat, I let out a frustrated grunt as Lavender, the bartender from the Saginaw chapter, sauntered in.

"What the fuck are you doing in this neck of the woods?" Warden spoke the words on my tongue.

"Keeping my options open," she winked, leaning her body over the table, giving us a view of her cleavage. "Besides, y'all are better to look at than the assholes in Saginaw."

Keeping my gaze on her face, no need to give her an ounce of hope of landing time with me. I had enough issues keeping up with Kira and her bullshit to add more trouble to the mix. "You realize this is a temporary position?"

"So is my bartending job, yet ten years later I'm still pouring beer four nights a week." She countered, popping her gum between her teeth.

"How does a temporary, part-time bartender transition into a receptionist slash accountant?"

"Same difference," Lavender shrugged. "Way I see it, I collect money for a service."

"And the bookkeeping?" Warden countered. "Hadn't heard the news you graduated from college."

Not bothering to hold back a laugh, I doubted Lavender graduated high school. Her attention glued to Linx's ball sack.

"I've balanced my checkbook since I was eighteen. Besides, I saw the computer system you have, probably does all the work for ya anyway."

Flipping her resumé over, I slid it into the no way in hell pile at the end of the table.

"We'll be in touch."

I speared my fingers into the hair at the crown of my head, the beginnings of a migraine trying to break through. Between listening to Kira bitch, keeping up with Club business, and trying to find out what Boom had up his sleeve, I was ready to crash.

Warden let out a high-pitched whistle, "Look at this one, brother."

Opening my eyes, I took the offered page, scanning the well-written resumé.

"Graduated from Michigan State majoring in Accounting with a minor in Criminal Justice. Top three-percent of her class." I nodded my head as I read aloud, seriously impressed with the person on paper.

"Send her in, Keys." Not bothering to lift my gaze, I couldn't help but wonder if this was a fabrication, copied straight out of a resumé book as I couldn't find a single typo.

"Gentlemen, this pretty lady is Emma Shaw."

Something in the way Keys said her name made me glance up. The sweet scent of apple pie floated under my nose as I watched Emma nervously take a seat.

Warden laid his arms on the table, balancing his chest against the muscles he'd worked so hard for.

"Why are you here?" His tone was clipped, and I watched Emma's eyes widen in surprise.

"I'm sorry?"

"With a resumé like yours," I waved the said document in the air, the apple pie scent growing stronger, oddly easing my headache. "There isn't a corporate door in one of those high-rises downtown you couldn't open. So please, Ms. Shaw, tell us why you are here?" Laying the page down, I crossed my arms over my chest.

I watched as she squared her shoulders, my gaze dropping to the tailored lines of her suit. Her corn silk hair reflected the light from the window beside her, light blue eyes boring into mine, then dropping down to the ink on my arms.

"I have no desire to work for one of those, as you say, corporate doors downtown."

Having known this Emma all of twelve seconds, I couldn't deny she intrigued me with the way she forged a tough front. I assumed, based on her impressive resumé and her conservative clothing, she wasn't accustomed to the grit she found in a room full of bikers.

"You realize this is a temporary position, less than a year in total?"

Nodding her head, "I do, which oddly is the amount of time I need to fill."

Moving to ask for clarification, Emma beat me to the punch as she layed those blue eyes on me.

"Sir."

"Hammer," I corrected. "Save the sir for someone who requires his dick to be measured."

"Mr. Hammer, I believe in honesty, and perhaps this will disqualify me for the position, but I've accepted a position with the IRS. Unfortunately, since the credentialing process can exceed a year, I need a position, such as the one you're offering, to tide me over until I can start my position in Chicago."

Shifting my gaze to Warden, we shared a look, silently telling the other hiring Emma could be the best thing we'd ever done, or land us back in jail.

"And you're okay with the salary? It's considerably lower than what a college—"

"It's better than zero, which is what I'm making now." She interrupted, her boldness stirring something deep inside.

"As you can see from the lobby full of applicants, we have many other individuals to interview."

"Of course," she nodded, but I could see the disappointment forming in her eyes. "I appreciate you taking the time to meet with me." When Emma stood to her full height, I followed suit, extending a hand to her.

"It was a pleasure," I nodded, holding onto her soft hand a little longer than necessary and watched her walk away as Keys escorted her out.

"It was a pleasure?" Warden mocked, scanning my face, looking for what I did not know. "The fuck was that?"

"She isn't like the other applicants, Warden. More like Bullet's mom."

Shifting in his seat, Warden tipped his chair back, a pensive look to his face.

"I think we should hire her. She's smart, pretty and, based on what I saw today, I suspect she could hold her own against some of our rougher personalities."

Nodding my head, I kept silent as I replayed our brief interaction in my head.

"I also think you should go get your family. We haven't heard shit from Boom or any of his Club. Besides, you're wound too tight, something I'm sure Kira could shake loose."

Letting out a humorless laugh, "I think we should at least check her references, make sure the shit she wrote is legit."

As if sensing her name was mentioned, my phone began to ring.

"You take care of that," Warden pointed at my phone. "And I'll make some calls, see if I can find any skeletons in Emma's closet."

My back ached as I pulled onto the dirt road, the overgrown vegetation much thicker than when I last visited. Maneuvering the cage around the bend, I noticed Stoney standing on the porch, his face more rigid than usual. After Kira's attack, Stoney offered to take her and my son to his cabin a few hours north of Detroit. The land was in his late wife's maiden name, untraceable to the SOC.

"Thank fuck you're here," Stoney stepped off the porch, greeting me as I opened the door. "I don't know how you can put up with—"

"Hammer, get the fuck in here now." Kira bellowed, interrupting Stoney, who waved his hand over his head as he straddled his Harley.

"Good luck, son. She's been in a mood since she woke up this morning." Stoney kicked his bike to life, leaving me unable to wish him a safe ride.

Climbing the steps, I caught the scent of Kira's perfume, an exotic fragrance most of the girls who hung around the Club wore.

Opening the screen door, I took in the rustic feel of the place. Stepping over the threshold, my gaze landed on Kira, her legs spread wide and her fingers rubbing her clit as if it were an Olympic sport.

"Get your pants off," she pointed at me with her free hand. "I need your dick, my fingers aren't cutting it anymore."

Scanning the room, I find a pile of Kira's belongings beside several toy trucks. "Where is Liam?"

"Asleep," she snapped, dipping her fingers into her cunt as she pulled at her nipple with the other. "Now get over here and fuck me."

It had been more than three months since I brought her here, ninety plus days of time to think about where I saw us. Things between Kira and I had been volatile for years, especially after I found out she'd fallen into bed with the man who'd tried to steal everything from me. She'd fed Angel information about the Club, resulting in false RICO charges and spending many months behind bars.

In the time she'd been gone, I found I'd missed the hell out of Liam, yet thoughts of having Kira back in my life left me with a strange pain in my chest. We needed to talk, set new boundaries for how things would be once she came back to Detroit. While the ever-horny side of me wanted nothing more than to slide my dick into her cunt, the sliver of rationality running inside me fueled me toward the pile of her belongings.

"Get dressed, Kira. We have a long drive ahead of us, and I've already had a shitty morning."

Moving to grab her bags, Kira sprang from her spot on the couch, placing her naked body in front of me.

"You aren't really turning me down." Batting her eyes, a move that used to put a smile on my face and gain the attention of my cock. "Remember how good it is between us?" Taking my hand in hers, Kira laid my hand over her left breast. Her skin felt warm, but the scent of her perfume stung my nose.

Dropping my hand to my side, I leveled my gaze with hers. "I remember a lot of shit, Kira. Some I bet you wished I'd forget." Stepping around her, "Now get dressed, if we hurry you can catch a shift at Distractions."

"Distractions, are you serious? Did you forget I was attacked there?"

Tossing Liam's bag over my shoulder, I took a step toward the door. "Daxx is running it now. Besides, how else are you going to pay for your nails and hair and shit?"

"That's it?" She cried. "All those years I stood beside you, and this is wha—"

"You made a choice," I roared. "When you opened your mouth and let Angel fuck my Club over, you kissed everything we had goodbye."

Kira rushed toward me, throwing her naked body against my back. "You don't mean that, Jon-"

"Don't you fucking dare," I rounded on her. "You may have spent your life on your knees sucking the dicks of men with short memories and getting what you want from them, but don't think for one second you can use my given name and everything you've done becomes water under the bridge. Nothing changed while you were away, Kira." The lie crossed my lips before I could contain it. Things had changed. I was a different man than I was a few months ago. I'd seen healthy relationships in my brothers, and this thing with Kira was as toxic as fuck.

"I'll say it one last time, get your ass dressed. We leave in five minutes."

Emma

CHAPTER
THREE

EMMA

THE SYMPHONY of the street greeted me as I pushed open the heavy door. *"We'll be in touch,"* resonated in my head as I tossed my bag onto the passenger seat of my car. Twisting my key in the ignition, I chanced a glance at the white aluminum building. "Who wants to work at a place like this anyway?" I mumbled out loud in an effort to cheer myself up. I'd known the second I walked into the room I was not getting the position.

I'd lied when Hammer asked me why I wasn't working in one of the high-rise buildings behind me. Truth was, those corporate doors wanted experience, something I was severely lacking. I'd kept books for the bar where my mother worked, experience I was regretting having eliminated from my resumé. Shifting my gaze to the rearview mirror, the pale blue eyes which held so much hope when I'd exited the car hours ago, were now dull with disappointment, the answer to my question swimming in the unshed tears rapidly forming.

"You do."

Taking a measured breath, I pulled into traffic. Crying never helped anything, a useless act which left you with a headache and ruined makeup. Having spent far too much of my life learning this lesson, I swallowed thickly and pushed down on the accelerator. As I turned into my apartment complex, my cell phone rang with my sister's tone, something I'd given her years ago when my studies took over my world. Where my life was filled with structure and responsibility, Macy jumped from one party to the next, dragging my nephew with her.

Shutting off my car, I considered letting her call go to voicemail, but as the ringing stopped and then resumed almost immediately, I knew this call involved money in one fashion or another.

"Hello."

"What the fuck are you doing?"

"Excuse me?"

"Not you," Macy snapped, and I heard the slur in her words. *"This fucking crotch goblin."*

Slamming my eyes shut, my heart ached for my nephew, Jackson. A sweet little boy trapped in a life he never asked for.

"Go sit the fuck down while I'm on the phone." I had to jerk the phone away from my ear due to the volume of her voice. Anger built in my chest as I imagined him flinching away.

"But I'm hungry, Mommy."

I heard Jackson plead in the background, opening my eyes wide as I reached for my wallet. Unlike my sister who had stopped maturing the day she became pregnant with Jackson, I would do anything, even put myself in debt, to make sure he was taken care of.

"Are you still living at the motel?" I asked as I put the call on speaker phone, opening the app I'd used the last time she called looking for money for groceries.

"What?"

"I said, are you still living at the motel?"

"Um, yeah, why?"

"'Cause I'm sending a delivery person with food for Jackson." I didn't even want to think about the filthy place she'd chosen to raise Jackson in, or the types of men he'd been exposed to.

"I don't need you to buy my kid food, Emma."

"I heard him, Macy. He said he was hungry."

"He ate a bag of popcorn, he's fine."

"When, Macy? Two days ago, three?" My sister had a history of forgetting to feed and bathe Jackson. Child services had stepped in once when a police officer found him sitting in a filthy diaper in the middle of the motel parking lot.

"*Don't tell me how to raise my fucking kid, bitch.*"

"Try doing it right, and I won't have to." I'd stopped holding my tongue when it came to my sister a long time ago, despite her threats to take him far away so I would never see him again.

"*Why don't you try having kids of your own? Oh, thats right, you fucking can't.*"

"There is a big difference between can't and choosing not to." I bit back as I entered my credit card information into the app. "Jackson's lunch will be there in fifteen minutes."

Grabbing my bag, I pulled the door open, hurrying up the sidewalk to my apartment.

"*Well, then I guess the new tenant will enjoy whatever you sent him because we are getting kicked out of here. I need four hundred bucks or we're on the streets.*"

Sliding my key into the lock, I twisted the door handle and stepped into my apartment. Tossing my bag on the table, I toed-off my shoes as I fell onto the cushions of the couch.

"Let me speak to the manager." I demanded, all-too familiar with the manipulations my sister was famous for. She'd bargained her way into more pockets than I cared to recall, using men, and women, for as much as she could shake from them.

"*He isn't here,*" she retorted, the sound of victory in her voice.

"The front desk attendant is fine," I countered, picturing her sitting in the center of an unmade bed, fingers buried in her unwashed hair.

"*Just wire me the fucking money, Emma.*" She screamed into my ear, an act I was way too accustomed to. "*Or tell me where you're living. We could come stay with you and Jackson could visit his favorite aunt.*"

I'd made the mistake of allowing my sister to cross the threshold of my door a few years ago. Her excessive partying and revolving door of men nearly got me kicked out of my apartment.

"If you're tru—"

"You're such a fucking cunt." She roared, interrupting me as usual before ending the call.

Lowering my cell phone, I tossed it to the cushion beside me, leaning my head back against the pillow. For the briefest of moments I considered calling the man Macy claimed was Jackson's father, asking him to take a ride out to the motel and check on things. However, doing so would bring on a level of trouble I'm not certain was worth the risk.

"Work isn't going to find itself," I reasoned out loud as I pushed myself off the couch and took a seat at my tiny kitchen table. Opening my laptop, I clicked on my email, silently hoping for a reply to one of the online applications I'd completed. Bracing my elbow on the table, I tucked my chin in my hand as I scrolled down the list of spam emails, finding nothing new. Releasing a depressed huff, I moved to open a new window when the sound of an incoming text shattered the silence. I was tempted to ignore it on the chance it's a colorful retort from my sister. Rising from the wooden chair, I grabbed my phone, not recognizing the number.

> Emma, your references checked out. The job is yours if you want it, Warden.

My hands shook as I read the message several times.

> Thank you, Mr. Warden. I most definitely want it.

My fingers were shaking with relief as I typed the words. Cringing as I instantly regretted the salutation I'd used.

> Glad to hear it. I'll meet you at eight in the morning.

Two men stood outside the building as I pulled my car into the same parking spot I'd occupied the day prior. Having been unable to sleep after receiving Warden's text, I was dressed and ready before the sun made its appearance.

Reaching for my bag, I plastered on a smile as I exited my car, taking several careful steps as I made my way to the front door.

"Mornin, darlin'. How can I help you?" The man closest to me questioned, his eyes doing a slow and deliberate once over. Moving to introduce myself, a gasp left my throat instead when a familiar deep voice sounded from my right.

"You fucking can't."

My attention shifted to the mountain of a man dressed similarly to the way he had yesterday. My gaze zeroed in on the set of hot pink lips tattooed on the side of his neck, then down to the patch with the word President written in block lettering on his vest.

"If you want to continue breathing, I'd suggest you get to work." Warden barked, causing me to flinch and the men to turn for the bay doors. I remained silent as he pulled out a set of keys, fluidly opening the door and silencing a beeping alarm before motioning me to enter.

The room looked somehow different as I stepped over the threshold. Where silent prayers of hope previously consumed my mind, a sense of purpose and endless possibilities took over.

"Here is your key," Warden held out the shiny gold key toward me, his calloused fingers brushing mine as he placed the piece of metal into my hand. "You need to think of a four digit code for the alarm. We each have a different number so we can track who comes and goes."

Touching the keypad, I entered the month and day of my graduation, sharing a genuine smile with Warden as I stepped further into the room.

"Your training will be baptism by fire I'm afraid. Syn, the girl you're covering for, has been put on strict bed rest and none of us knows shit about her system."

Looking around, I noticed a large desk against the far wall, the top covered in stacks of paper and beauty products. On the opposite side was a half wall, the top made of glass or plastic, overlooking the shop where several cars were suspended in the air. To my left was a bank of metal cabinets, stacked high with bankers boxes. Judging by the layers of dust, neither had been used in a long time.

"Where are the computers?"

Warden pointed at the single monitor in the room. "The boys use this old thing to look up parts. Syn preferred paper, so the system we bought a few years ago is stuffed in the closet over there."

Following the direction he pointed, I crossed the room, opening a tiny door beside the metal cabinets.

"Are you kidding me?" I exclaimed as my gaze landed on the system I'd spent the last four years earning my degree with. "Do you have any idea what this baby can do?" I questioned over my shoulder.

"No," Warden adjusted his stance, his brows furrowing as he twisted the key ring between his fingers. "Listen, Emma, I have a pile of shit waiting for me across the lot." He nodded in the direction we'd come from. "This is your space. The guys," pointing behind him. "Know not to mess with you. Feel free to do whatever you want with what's in the closet. You can stuff Syn's shit in a box or toss it in the dumpster, doesn't make a difference to me. There are only two rules you need to know if you want to keep your job. One, repeat not one goddamn thing you hear in this office. Two, I don't give two shits if the building is on fire, never open that door over there." Ticking off each item on his fingers, I turned my head to look out the window beside me, catching sight of the single door on the side of the building across the parking lot.

"Work hours are eight to five, you get an hour for lunch. I need the men paid every Friday, as well as yourself. You'll find petty cash in the drawer along with the checkbook to pay the bills. Use the cash for lunch or whatever, I don't care. If you need me, call the number I used to text you, but don't give it out. Any questions?"

"No," I lied. A myriad of questions flooded my mind, although I knew to the depths of my soul I would need to figure them out on my own.

"Hammer will be in later. He'll need to put you on the accounts."

"It's fine, I'm sure Syn kept everything up to date." What an odd name I thought to myself. Was it her given name or something Warden and Hammer gifted her?

A sense of unease blanketed my body as I watched Warden cross the lot and disappear through the door he'd warned me to avoid. My limited experience with bikers told me that was the sacred place they called Church, where they held their secret meetings.

Turning back to the room, I headed straight for the closet, dropping to my knees and breaking the seal on the first box. I felt like a kid on Christmas morning as I stared at the contents. Looking over my shoulder, I took in the mess covering the desk. "Not going to clean itself, Emma," I said aloud as I jumped to my feet and crossed the room.

Three hours, and several paper cuts later, I closed the lid of the last box I'd filled with Syn's personal items. When Warden mentioned they didn't know her system, I bet he had no idea she didn't either, as there was no rhyme or reason to the calamity I'd sorted through. The drawers were filled with nail polish, empty perfume bottles, and several pieces of ripped panties. What I'd assumed were business receipts, in reality were bills I had no idea whether paid or not. Having stacked them in order by date, I made a mental note to contact the companies once I had the new program set up.

"I see you're settling in just fine."

Startled, I spun around to face the voice, knocking the box containing the Bluetooth scanner to the floor in the process.

"I'm so—"

"Careful."

Hammer and I spoke in unison, our fingers brushing as we both reached for the fallen box. An odd, yet welcomed chill ran up my arm, causing me to gasp and a smile to form on Hammer's lips.

"Allow me." His deep voice stirred something inside me, his dark eyes possessing a level of intensity which caused my mouth to run dry. *Was he this handsome yesterday?* I silently asked myself, cataloging his masculine features, paying special attention to the sharpness of his jawline.

"I see you've been busy." His compliment pulled me out of my lustful haze, a place I had no business visiting. Given his devilish good looks, and well-established bad boy persona, I suspected he sifted through women like grains of sand, never taking the time to distinguish one from another.

"Yes." Standing to my full height, I moved around the desk, placing the wooden structure between Hammer and myself. "I hope to have everything up and running before I leave tonight."

Hammer surveyed the piles I'd created. "Warden mentioned your excitement over the boxes in the closet. I take it you're familiar with the system?"

Nodding, "Just wait until I have the whole thing set up. I'll have you asking yourself why you'd left it hidden in a closet this whole time."

Hammer's smile increased as he took several steps toward the door, "Of that, I have no doubt." He winked as he opened the door and stepped into the parking lot.

As the clock on the wall neared five o'clock, I blew a wayward strand of hair out of my face. It had taken all day, but I'd met my goal and managed to assemble all the monitors and connected the program to the internet. Tomorrow I would show the men in the garage how to use the scanners, call the companies listed on the bills and find out where the accounts stood. If my progression continued, I'd have SOC Towing automated by the end of the week. Moving to log off my computer, the shrill sound of a voice stopped me in my tracks.

"Who in the fuck are you and where is Syn?"

Hammer

CHAPTER
FOUR
HAMMER

WARMTH ENVELOPED me as the comforts of sleep tried to hang on. Clinging to the edge of my dream as it disappeared into the mist of a new day. A smile tickled my lips as I thought of the more intimate points of the faceless girl who'd invaded my sleep.

"You like that, baby?"

My cock swelled at the memory, the feel of her soft lips slipping over the head and down the shaft, her warm tongue swirling around the tender flesh.

"God, you're so fucking big."

Clarity rushed forward as the voice became familiar, my eyes snapping open to find Kira positioned between my legs, her fist wrapped around my cock, as the head disappeared into her mouth.

"What the fuck?" I demanded, the fire in my words dying off as the sensation took over, my body craving a release. Reaching down, my fingers combing through her silky locks. Kira may be a manipulative bitch, but she could suck a dick like a seasoned pornstar.

"Lay still, baby, you need this as much as I do." She purred, flattening her tongue and running it from base to tip.

She wasn't wrong. With the increased stress in my world, I've had little time to indulge in the pleasures only a woman could provide.

Reaching into my nightstand I pulled out a sleeve of condoms, ripping the top one open.

"Let me," Kira's hand covers mine.

"Not on your fucking life," I jerked out of her clutches. I wouldn't trust Kira any further than I could throw her. "This changes nothing," I clarified, slipping the latex on my swollen cock. "This isn't us getting back together." Springing to my knees, I flipped her over, diving my arm under her pelvis to raise her ass in the air. I didn't have to question if she's ready, Kira was always ready, something I used to find appealing in her. "You're a step above a Club whore," I reminded her as I slipped my cock into her, gripping her hips as I moved in search of my release. "And we both know how many of those I've done this to," I whispered into her ear as my orgasm rushed forward.

"Did you get Kira settled in?"

Nodding, my gaze flashed to Raiden."Dropped her off before I came in. Thanks for offering up your rental." Yesterday, as I was leaving to go collect Kira and my son, Raiden and Daxx pulled into the lot, returning from a protection run. Raiden recently moved Erin into a new house he'd purchased for her, leaving the rental she'd lived in vacant.

"That's what family is for, brother." Raiden slapped me on the back before taking his place at the table. "Besides, it made Mrs. Flowers' day when I asked her if she was interested in watching Liam."

Warden burst through the door as I was taking my seat, several of my brothers rushing in behind him. An uneasy feeling settled in my stomach as I took in the heaviness in his features.

"Listen up; we hired a young woman to fill in until Syn comes back after her maternity leave."

Shifting my gaze to the faces around the table, I watched as several shifted uncomfortably in their seats, with the exception of a few. Syn had made her rounds, fucking the majority of us on the regular. When it came out she was pregnant, a number of us became nervous. While I wouldn't mind more children, I wasn't ready to go through the level of hell I had when Kira gave birth to Liam.

"Is she hot?" Daxx spouted off.

"She's off limits is what she is," I said before Warden could, my tone serious and unwavering.

"Claiming two chicks, are we, Hammer?" Daxx wiggled his brows as he tilted his chair back on two legs.

"Her name is Emma Shaw and she was here and ready to work before most of you motherfuckers finished playing with your morning wood." Warden spoke from my left, putting an end to Daxx and his unique brand of humor.

"I've spoken with the guys in the shop and now I'm telling the rest of you. Emma is not a hang around and you're not to treat her as such."

Several heads nodded around the table, but I could see the curiosity floating in as many eyes. We're a rugged bunch, accustomed to taking what we wanted, when we wanted it.

"I got a call from Kannon earlier," Warden's confession pulled my attention back to him. An unease filled my stomach as I stared at his hardened features. "Boom was arrested in Ann Arbor last night."

Snapping my gaze to Chopper, "Who does your brother know in Ann Arbor?" Chopper chose to remain in Detroit, said he wanted to put down roots and join a real Club. Keys had taken him under his wing, not because they were instant friends, but because he didn't completely trust him.

"No one that I know of."

My mind flashed to Emma's resumé and the city mentioned on it. I hadn't questioned if she had family in the area, or if there was another reason for her being in Detroit.

Kannon walked through the door, forcing me to push the question to the back of my mind. I'd drive by her address later, see if I could find anything suspicious.

Locking gazes with Kannon, "Do we know why Boom was arrested?"

Spinning a chair in the corner around, Kannon straddled the seat, resting his arms along the back. "Cops were called when a fight broke out at one of those dive bars offering cheap beer to broke college kids.

According to the report, Boom took a swing at one of the responding officers. When they ran him, they found a bench warrant for a parole violation."

Chopper tipped his head back in laughter, "Boom has a thing for nerdy girls, always has." Snapping his gaze to Kannon, "Sorry, man, no disrespect."

Since bringing Hailey back from Chicago, Kannon had worked over-time convincing her he was be the kind of man she could trust.

"If you're referring to Hailey, none taken. She's fucking gorgeous, not a nerdy thing about her."

I didn't bother to argue. Hailey was much like Erin and Jillian in her dress and mannerisms. I've learned it's better to respect a brother's decision in who he puts his patch on than to argue she's his polar opposite.

"He has this thing he does where he finds the most uncomfortable looking girl in the room. You know, the one who was more than likely dragged to the bar by her well-meaning friends. He has a sixth-sense about it, able to pick out the poor girl with a hidden desire for a trip on the wild side. If I know my brother, punching the cop was his twisted way to garner the attention of his next victim."

Kannon cleared his throat, "Want me to have a look at the security cameras? See if we can find his target?"

"Nah," Warden declined. "We can't exactly go knocking on the poor girl's door and risk gaining some unwanted attention. Let me know when his court appearance is. May have to send a few of you to Ann Arbor to pay his bail."

Kannon nodded before standing. "I hate to cut this short, but I promised Hailey I'd go to the oral surgeon with her."

Once Hailey had settled in and began working for Kannon, Jody, his assistant, befriended her. The pair had become thick as thieves. When Hailey confided in Jody about wanting to have her overbite fixed, but lacked the courage and the money to have the procedure done, Jody told Kannon, who had called a surgeon Doc Ash recommended, writing him a check for the lion's share of the cost.

"You sure you want to have her teeth fixed, Kannon?"

"Daxx," I warned, being in no mood to break up another fight between the two.

"All I was going to say was, she's smoking hot now. Imagine the attention she'll get with a new smile."

Kannon stood to his full height, a wicked smile splitting his face. "Even if she changed her mind, she'll still be the hottest woman I know." Moving behind Daxx's seat, "And way fucking out of your league."

A collective hush fell over the room as we waited for Kannon to pounce on Daxx, but as he twisted the knob and stepped out of the room, Warden turned back to the table.

"Any news on Cavanagh or Milania?"

Raiden laid his phone on the table, his gaze shifting between myself and Warden. "Not a peep from the Cavanagh's, or the Graziano's for that matter, which considering, is odd as fuck."

Something definitely wasn't right there. Milania was the only daughter of a mafia boss in Boston, yet there was no mention of her disappearance and subsequent request for recovery.

"Milania hasn't touched her credit cards or bank account. Daxx and I checked on her apartment during this last run and found it empty. The management company said they put what little belongings there were in the trash when she failed to pay rent."

Turning my attention toward Warden, I watched as he stared off into the distance, the thoughts running through his mind evident on his face.

"If there's nothing else," he paused, allowing each man in the room the opportunity to speak. When the room remained silent, Warden tapped his fingers on the wood and stood to his feet, effectively ending Church.

Stepping over the threshold, I found Stoney in his usual spot behind the bar.

"Met your new girl," he called as he wiped down the counter, keeping his focus on the white towel in his hand.

"And?"

"I like her. She isn't Syn, mind you, but I like her."

"Glad you approve, old man." I tossed over my shoulder. Stoney had a soft spot for most of the hang-arounds, except for Kira.

As I stepped into the parking lot, the sight that greeted me had me stopping in my tracks. Emma had the hood of her car open, her ass sticking straight in the air as she searched for something. Clearing the distance, I kept my gaze on the rounded globes of her ass, appreciating the way the denim of her jeans hugged her curves.

"Need some help?" I called when I reached the halfway point in an effort not to scare her for a second time today.

"Yes...no. Ugh, I don't know." She huffed, tossing what looked to be her keys to the ground.

Picking up her keys, I moved to stand beside her, shifting my gaze from the way-past vintage motor to the adorable owner.

"I just had the thing rebuilt last month. The guy swore to me I would get another hundred-thousand miles out of her."

Offering the discarded keys to her, "What's it doing?"

Emma shifted her gaze to me, searching my face for the briefest of moments before taking several steps back. "It's nothing, I'll call the guy." She trailed off as she reached into her purse and pulled out her phone. I knew without asking, someone had said or done something to spook her.

"Emma, you work for a towing company, which is attached to a mechanic shop." I pointed at the marquee above the bay doors. "Now, tell me what the problem is."

Shaking her head, "I have a warranty, and...and she said—"

"Who upset you, darlin'?" The question was rhetorical as I could practically smell the lingering scent of Kira's cheap perfume.

"No one, it's fine," she tried to wave me off. "I have a bus pass." Emma moved to close the hood, but I slammed my hand against the rusting metal.

"I don't give two shits about a bus pass. I asked who upset you?"

Dropping her gaze to the concrete beneath our feet, my anger growing by the second. "Your wife came by and made it clear she wasn't comfortable with me working here. Said if I wanted to keep my job, I needed to stay away from you."

Placing my index finger under her chin, I tilted her face up toward mine. "I'm not married," I said with conviction. "I have a son with the woman who lied to you."

"How did you—?"

"Kira is the master of manipulation," I cut her off, moving my hand to cup her jaw.

Emma shook her head, dislodging my hand from her face. Standing my ground, I lowered my hand, but remained close.

"Clearly you haven't met my sister," Emma let out an adorable scoff.

"Got a storyteller in the family, do ya?"

The smile she shared with me earlier sprung to life. Finding I enjoyed it so much, I cataloged it to memory.

"Macy wouldn't know the truth if it shook her hand and introduced itself."

"Must make holidays a real treat," I added from experience, remembering the fight which broke out between my sister and Kira last Thanksgiving.

"I ugh," Emma stammered, then looked off into the distance. "My family isn't exactly the holiday celebrating type."

"Well, you're in luck, my sister, Layla, is the queen of potlucks. Which comes in handy since SOC loves any excuse to have a party." Making a mental note to call Layla as soon as I got Emma settled.

"Now, tell me what's wrong with your car." Hooking my hands on my hips, I nodded my head toward the pile of metal.

"When I turn the key, nothing happens. My dash stays black and the engine silent."

"Could be your battery." I reached for the terminals, jiggling the cables.

"The battery is new, the guy who rebuilt the engine said it was best to replace it."

Nodding my head in agreement. "Tell you what," dusting my hands off and closing the hood. "Let me have the guys put it on the lift, run a few diagnostics."

Emma immediately began shaking her head. "Warden sent them all home, said to meet him at a place called Bullet's bar."

Moving to walk around her, I placed my hands on her shoulders. "Don't move, I need to grab something."

Jogging into the office, I grabbed the key to the car I kept at the shop.

"Here, use this for as long as you need." Pointing the key fob at the white car next to Emma's, the lights flashing and alarm beeping.

"You can't be serious?" Emma laughed, her eyes wide as she pointed to the car.

"Got something against German engineering?" I prodded, holding the key toward her.

"No, but I can't drive a Mercedes."

"Why? It's an automatic, like yours."

"It's also more expensive than mine."

Gripping her shoulders once again, I bent my knees, bringing myself eye level with her. "You need a car, I have an extra one. It's insured and a hell of a lot safer than the one you pulled up in."

I watched as a war raged in Emma's blue eyes, the longing to drive the luxury car versus being the independent girl she prided herself on.

"Fine, but only until we figure out what's wrong with my car."

I waited until Emma pulled into traffic, the taillights of my car disappearing into the Detroit night before pulling out my cell.

"Hey, it's Hammer. See what you can dig up on Emma Shaw, specifically a sister by the name of Macy."

Emma

CHAPTER
FIVE
EMMA

"IT'S AN EASY FIX, the issue is getting the parts."

Gripping the keys to Hammer's car in my fist, I struggled to keep my composure. This wasn't the first time I'd heard those words passing through the lips of a mechanic, the gentleman who'd rebuilt my engine mentioned the same issue.

"Given the age of your car, it could take a few weeks."

Nodding, I lowered my head, rounding my desk and dropping my purse to the floor. Having tossed and turned for the majority of the night, my mind fixed on the safety of the borrowed luxury car parked in the lot outside my bedroom window, I was running on fumes. As soon as the sun came up, I'd gotten dressed and driven back to the shop, finding my car on the lift, and a concerned looking Cisco wiping his hands. He shared how Hammer called him, telling him to have a look at my car and fix it. I'd argued I had a warranty with the rebuilt engine. However he'd dashed my hopes when he explained the part that had given way would not be covered as it wasn't a part of the engine.

"What about a salvage yard?"

Shrugging, Cisco leveled his gaze with mine. "It's an option, but not something I would recommend as you wouldn't be able to tell if the electrical components have been exposed to the elements or not. If it were my car," he pointed over his shoulder. "I wouldn't chance it failing and being stranded."

Cisco was right. I'd been lucky my car broke down where it did, I didn't want to think of this happening on the interstate, or one of the side roads I'd used to get around the city.

"I'll go ahead and order the part." A triumphant smile splitting his face in half. "Gives me an excuse to play with the program you installed yesterday."

"I don't—" I began to argue, worried, based on the numbers I'd seen on receipts yesterday, I wouldn't be able to afford the repair. Cisco's raised hand stole the confession from my lips.

"Hammer will beat my ass if I don't. So please, Emma, let me do my job."

Sending a small prayer the delivery would indeed take weeks, I shared a smile and nodded in affirmation.

I watched as Cisco walked through the metal door, lowered my car and then towed it around the edge of the building. Gazing into the still empty parking lot, I wrapped my arms around myself in an effort to keep from falling apart. Driving home last night, I'd allowed myself to sink into the buttery leather of Hammer's car, a wave of guilt flooding me with an image of Macy and Jackson sleeping on the street while I was warm and dry. When I tried to call her, a man answered the phone, told me Macy was busy and hung up.

As I moved from the window, a Jeep and a lifted truck pulled into the parking lot, taking the spots on either side of Hammer's Mercedes. A beautiful brunette stepped from the truck, her smile wide as she rounded the front of the Jeep joining the raven-haired driver.

Assuming they were customers dropping off a vehicle for repair, I hurried back to my desk, donning the best smile I could conjure. Transferring the appointments from the tattered calendar Syn used to the computer was on my to-do list. Now, as I watched the women walk through the door, I regretted not coming in when sleep failed to find me last night and completing the task.

"Can I help you?"

"You must be Emma?"

"Yes?" I answered cautiously, rising from my seat, my eyes darting back and forth between the pair.

"You don't remember me, do you?"

Tilting my head to the side, I scanned my memory for any recollection. "You look familiar," I admitted, unable to place her pretty face.

"I'm Erin, one of the nurses at the Clinic." She smiled brightly, offering her outstretched hand to me.

"That's right, I remember now." Returning the smile, taking her hand and gently shaking it.

"How's the ear?" She asked, pointing toward my left side.

"Much better, thank you. Do you have an appointment?" Reaching for the calendar laying on my desk.

"Not really, no," Erin shook her head. "We're not here about our cars, though."

"Oh?" I questioned, staring at Erin through confused eyes.

"We're here to see you." The raven hair woman added, the smile on her face making me uneasy.

"Me?" My open palm landed in the center of my chest.

"Forgive me," Erin began, placing her body between myself and the dark-haired woman. "This is Jillian, one of my best friends and Bullet's girlfriend."

Shifting my gaze back to Jillian, I wondered if the boyfriend and the bar Warden mentioned last night had any correlation.

"Pleasure to meet you, Jillian. Although I don't recall meeting anyone by the name of Bullet."

Jillian waved her hand toward me, "Oh, you'd know if you'd met Bullet. It's hard to miss his booming personality." Her eyes grew wide, a smile crossing her lips at what I safely assumed was the mental image of the man in question.

The pair burst into laughter, leaning into one another as they enjoyed their private joke. Stepping to the side, I dropped my attention to my desk, scanning it for a way out of the conversation. Erin and Jillian didn't strike me as being anything like Kira, who'd dropped by yesterday. However, by Erin's admission, they were affiliated with members of the Club, and in my experience, those types of women were all the same.

"You said you were here to see me?" I spoke loud enough to end their giggles.

"Sorry, Emma," Jillian apologized, appearing to struggle to compose herself. "You'll have to forgive Erin and I. We bonded surprisingly well from the moment we were introduced by our men."

"Which is the main reason we're here," Erin said as she looked at Jillian, their shared expressions much different this time, more get-to-the-point and less high school cliquing.

"Go on," I encouraged, eager to learn the answer as I leaned my hip against the wood of my desk.

"Last night when Raiden and Bullet came home, they mentioned the new girl who was working while Syn was on bed rest."

Shaking my head, I pushed away from the desk, a fire I'd long ago extinguished sparking to life. "And you thought you'd come down and what? Size up the new girl? Draw clear boundaries where your boyfriends are concerned? I'll tell you like I told your other friend, I'm here to work, not get involved with any of the men here."

"More like take you to lunch and get to know you," Jillian retorted, her voice lacking the slightest hint of dishonesty.

Shocked at the abrupt turn of the conversation, my mouth opened and closed several times as my gaze drifted between the two women.

"Why?" The question left my lips of its own accord.

"Because, according to Raiden and Bullet, you are a college grad, same as the both of us. Which is something of a rarity in the women around here. Now, grab your purse—"

"I have work to do," I interrupted, dropping into my chair and directing my attention at the screen. "Perhaps—"

"Work can wait," Erin snapped, reaching across my desk and turning off my monitor. "Now, grab your purse before I call Warden."

A smile tugged at my lips as Jillian pulled into a parking spot outside the Twenty-Third Street diner. It was the newest restaurant in the downtown area, and given the hour of the day, was packed to the rafters.

"Come on, Emma, I'm starving." Jillian called to me as she opened the driver's side door and exited the Jeep. Sliding from the back seat, I joined the pair as they walked through the front door, the taste of victory almost overpowering the mouth-watering aroma billowing from the restaurant.

Inside was, as suspected, crowded and chaotic, not an empty seat to be had.

"Ladies," a deep voice called from behind the counter. "Connie is waiting for you in the Snug."

My heart dropped as the term slipped from the man's lips, surprised to hear of the existence of such a place in a diner, and an available table.

"Thanks," Erin waved to the man, making her way to the back of the restaurant. My shoes felt as if they were made of lead as I followed her down the aisle. I caught the stares of several patrons, sharing their curiosity as to who these women were.

"You're the guest, so you get to pick which side you want to sit on." Erin offered, pointing to the table in the corner revealed by a sliding door. Glancing at Erin's smiling face, I dropped to the closest bench, scooting to the window as fast as I could.

A glass of water appeared in front of me, followed by a laminated menu and rolled silverware.

"Special today is a reuben sandwich with fries for five bucks, or the soup for a dollar more."

Drifting my gaze to the owner of the voice, my eyes landed on who I assumed was Connie. Bright red hair, too vibrant to come from nature, warred with the deep shade of her lipstick. Given the amount of lines surrounding her lips, I imagined she was either in her sixties, or a chain smoker.

"Do you like nachos, Emma?"

Snapping my gaze to Jillian who sat across from me, I nodded my head absently.

"I was hoping you'd say that. Erin and I love to eat appetizers as our main meals."

I sat silently as she turned toward Connie. "Ask Darryl to make us one of his famous nacho plates."

"Half chicken and half beef," Jillian added, her gaze snapping to mine, brows bending. "You're not a vegetarian are you?"

"No," I muttered, slightly intimidated by the situation.

"Oh good," she smiled. "Not that anything's wrong with it if you were, it just makes things easier to order if you're not." She winked a second before her gaze drifted to something or someone behind me.

"Over here," she waved her hand over her head, forcing me to look over my shoulder. Coming up the aisle, as if a model during fashion week, was a tall woman dressed in fishnet stockings under the tiniest pair of bootie shorts I'd ever seen. Her top barely held in the double-d breasts of hers, the stripes in her dark hair matching the hot pink lace adorning her top.

"Hey girl," Ms. Bootie Shorts spoke, placing a kiss to Jillian's cheek as she slid into the seat beside her.

"Emma, this is my friend Roxie." Jillian tipped her head toward the woman. "Roxie, this is—"

"Emma Shaw," Roxie finished for her. "The Club's new pride and joy," she added, a sharp bite coating her tone.

"Roxie." Jillian cautioned, a weighted tension settling over the table.

"What?" Roxie demanded. "Syn is going to need her job back after the baby is born. If this chick is as good as Warden says, Syn doesn't stand a chance."

Moving to open my mouth to argue, my retort died on my tongue as a timid voice sounded from the end of the table.

"Sorry I'm late." The newcomer announced as she slid onto the bench beside Erin.

"You're right on time, Hailey," Erin said as she wrapped an arm around the girl, giving her a warm hug. "How are you feeling?"

Scanning as much of Hailey as I could see, trying to hide my perusal so as not to appear creepy. She had slight bruising on the edges of her cheeks, and noticeable swelling where her jaw and ear connected.

"My jaw is really sore, other than that, I'm fine."

Dropping my gaze to the menu, I tried not to assume where the bruises had come from. Closing my eyes, I tried to shove away the memories of a time Macy had similar marks on her face, a gift for opening her mouth to the wrong man.

"I told you there was nothing to worry about," Erin said as Connie sat a steaming bowl of what looked to be soup in front of Hailey, the action returning my attention to the far side of the table

"Hailey was born with a severe overbite, one she's finally in a position to do something about."

Shifting my attention back to Hailey, I shared a genuine smile, grateful the bruising wasn't the result of abuse.

"I knew a girl in college who had to have a similar procedure after she hit her mouth on her steering wheel during a car accident."

While I could recall with perfect clarity the hushed conversation which occurred in the row below me in my statistics class, I couldn't, however, remember the girl's name.

"Was this one of your sorority sisters?" Roxie's snippy tone slashed deep within me.

"I had neither the money nor the desire to pledge a sorority." The retort was out of my mouth before my brain could engage.

"Seriously, Roxie?"

I ignored the plea from my right, instead, centering my gaze upon the thick-lash rimmed eyes opposite me. "As to your earlier accusation, I'm no one's pride and joy, just a simple girl who took advantage of a dozen scholastic benefactors in order to gain an education. It is not now, nor will it ever be, my intention to steal Syn's job. For the record, I have a six-figure job waiting for me once she returns."

Drifting my gaze around the room, an ember of fire sparked inside my chest. "I have no desire to hook up with any of your men, no hidden agenda to trick one of them into patching me as their property." I said adamantly as I reached for my purse. "While this charade of an invitation has been—"

"How are you familiar with that term?" Hailey interrupted me from the end of the table, her brows severely bent in confusion. Of all the women at this table, I'd felt most drawn to her. While I knew next to nothing about her, I suspected we were cut from the same cloth.

"Television, like everyone else." I lied, motioning for Erin to let me out of the booth. Having neither the energy nor the desire to travel down that road with this group.

"Please don't go," Hailey's plea stopped me in my tracks. "I'm sorry for upsetting you, it's just I've..." she trailed off and I could hear the tremble in her voice, biting into my soul.

"No, Hailey," Roxie's voice cut the building tension. "Don't you dare say it." Roxie slammed her hand on the table, "Don't you dare say his fucking name."

Dropping back onto the bench, I watched as Erin wrapped her arms around Hailey, my curiosity off the charts as to the backstory.

"Warden and Kannon are working their asses off to find that prick and his little bitches."

"I didn't know you spent so much time with Warden."

Returning to my place beside the window, grateful for Hailey's deflection. I now understood the root of Roxie's hostility. Just like Kira, she needed to mark her territory, something completely unnecessary as I saw Warden as my employer and nothing else.

"It's casual," Roxie shrugged her shoulders as Connie placed a large platter of food in the center of the table.

"It's not Daxx, it is what it is." Jillian said before shoving a loaded chip into her mouth and I'm not sure I wanted to know the story behind her clipped words.

"Speaking of Kannon, how are things going with the two of you?"

Hailey lifted her spoon, blowing across the steaming soup, her gaze focused on the wood grains of the table. "It's complicated."

"Really?" Roxie reached for a chip, wrapping an errant string of cheese around her finger. "Kannon is a great guy."

"You don't have to sell him, Roxie. I know how wonderful and generous he is." Hailey admitted as she returned the spoon to the bowl. My heart broke for Hailey as I watched a single tear trickle down her pale cheek.

"Would you look at how rude we've all been." Erin spoke as she passed out plates around the table. "Here we invited Emma to lunch to get to know her better, and then carry on as if she knows everything we're talking about."

Glancing at my watch, "It's fine, Erin. I have to get back to work anyway. Hammer will be angry—"

"Hammer is the one who asked us to take you out."

"What?"

Erin leaned against the table. "He's afraid Kira may have rattled your cage when she showed up the other night."

Leaning my head back, I let out a measured breath as the memory of Kira's visit surfaced.

She'd come into the shop, dressed much like Roxie, minus the fishnet stockings. She'd been direct, labeling Hammer as her husband and father of their two year old son. She'd boasted how they keep their marriage spicy by making each other jealous in the pursuit of other people. As she'd made to leave, she'd told me not to set my sights on Hammer, sharing his immense thirst for women and how they'd invited a few of his conquests into their marital bed.

"It will take more than an angry wife to scare me off."

"They aren't married," Hailey admitted as she sniffed in the final remnants of her tears.

"I know," I nodded. "Hammer told me."

"Kira used to be one of my best friends," wiping her mouth with a paper napkin, Roxie turned her attention to the passing cars outside the window. "She's too selfish to be married, too wrapped up in her own needs to worry about anyone else's." Shifting her gaze back toward me, "Especially Liam's."

The tension from earlier shifted to something different, something more unified, yet unspoken.

"Our Jillian, who is practically married to Bullet," Erin began, her cheerful voice piercing the uncomfortable bubble surrounding the table. "Is a successful business owner."

"Oh my god. We are not practically married." Jillian laughed, the tips of her fingers circled the ring finger of the opposite hand, a movement I doubted she was aware of. "The business owner is correct, and thankfully I've been busy enough to hire two groomers this year."

"That's quite an accomplishment considering nearly half of all small businesses fail within the first year." The statistical quote was out of my mouth before I could stop it. Turning toward Jillian, "I'm so sorry."

"And Hailey here," Erin continued, completely ignoring my verbal diarrhea. "Is one of the finest attorneys in the state of Michigan. Who happens to have the undivided attention of our resident esquire, Kannon."

I appreciated what Erin was attempting to do, no doubt her skills of deflection played a huge part in her success as a nurse. I smiled as Hailey used her index finger to push her black-rimmed glasses up her nose, the apple of her cheeks reddening with embarrassment.

"And Roxie is not only Jillian's best friend, she is also the best hair stylist in the Detroit metro area."

I watched as pride covered Roxie's face, momentarily cracking the tough girl facade. I could practically feel it radiating off her. While I didn't appreciate her callousness, I certainly joined her in the feeling of self-accomplishment.

"That is when she isn't fucking my husband."

Snapping my gaze to the woman standing at the end of the table, her lips pursed and dark eyes filled with enough determination to make me uncomfortable.

"This is SOC property, you're not supposed to be here, Farrah."

"It's okay, Hailey." Roxie reassured, her lack of intimidation evident in the confident way she held eye contact with the newcomer. "Besides, what's good for the goose is even better for the gander." Crossing her arms over her ample chest, Roxie nodded toward the man standing a few feet behind Farrah. "You gave up the right to your opinion on who Warden takes to his bed when you started fucking Detective Dickhead over there."

My nerves went into overdrive as Farrah balanced her hands on the table, keeping her gaze trained on Roxie. She was a beautiful woman, with an ample chest which rivaled Roxie's, dark hair and intimidating eyes.

"I didn't come here to talk about Warden's shriveled dick." Farrah's voice dropped to a level which sent a chill over my body, giving me the perspective that this woman was perfectly suited for Warden.

"Farrah, you know what your problem is? You are drowning in regret, pissed at yourself for not realizing the reason the grass appears greener on the other side is because it's fertilized with bullshit."

I held my breath as I waited for either a string of expletives, or the table to be tossed with the spark of a fight.

"You're cocky as fuck, Roxie, something I've always admired in you. However, don't fool yourself, little girl, Warden will send you packing the second I ask him to."

The mood at the table shifted as Farrah's words wiped the confidant smirk off Roxie's face. I suspected the pair had been friends at some point in the past, their relationship—like many in the MC world, severed because of a man.

"I didn't come here to start a fight."

"Then why did you?" Erin's tired voice broke the tension, my gaze shifting to her annoyed face.

"We need to talk."

Hammer

CHAPTER
SIX
HAMMER

"DON'T WORRY ABOUT A THING," my sister assured Bullet as she took the wad of cash from his hand. I watched as she sprinted away before he could pull it back. "I'll give you the perfect party to pop the question," she tossed over her shoulder before jumping into her car.

My sister Layla had missed her calling when she chose to become a psychologist instead of an event planner. From the time she came into the world, she'd possessed the ability to turn a lot of nothing into something beautiful. Farrah may be the unofficial planner for the Club, but Layla had all the talent.

Walking over, I laid my hand on Bullet's shoulder. "Never thought I'd see the day when Bullet McKnight handed his balls to a woman."

With a humorless laugh, "Neither did I, brother." Bullet turned his gaze toward me. "A good woman will do that to ya."

Hooking my hands on my hips, I silently nodded in agreement. I'd seen firsthand how my father adored my mother, her loyalty and devotion allowing him to go out and earn a good living for our family. He'd taught Layla never to settle for anything less than she deserved, thus the reason she was still single. Too bad I'd failed to listen when he gave me the same lesson on choosing a mother for my children.

"You don't have to sell me, man. I know there are good women out there." *I just haven't found one yet*, I added inside of my head.

"Speaking of good women, Kannon get back to you yet?"

After Kira showed her ass with Emma, I'd pulled Kannon to the side and asked him if he had any news on the status of my petition to terminate Kira's parental rights. She'd shown nothing but disdain when it came to the treatment of our son. Liam deserved the best of everything, even if it meant the lack of a mother in his life.

"Nah, he said by the end of the—" The shrill ring of my cell halted the completion of my sentence. "Who the fuck?" Not recognizing the number, I nearly ignored it when my curiosity got the better of me.

"Hello?"

"Hey, Hammer, it's Cisco. Sorry to bother you, but we have a situation down here and I can't get Daxx on the phone."

My gaze flashed to Bullet's face whose bent brow told me he'd heard the conversation.

"He's at the doctor's office with Syn, what's up?"

"It's uh..." Cisco faded off and I knew what he was about to say without hearing it. *"It's Kira, man. She's pissed off and tearing up the place."*

Tilting my head back, I let out a strained breath as I squeezed my eyes shut. The first time I'd laid eyes on her was during a trip to Chicago. She was kicking the shit out of two girls as I had entered the room. I remember watching as she'd wailed on these two girls, clothes and blood flying in a million directions. Once the fight was over, I'd motioned for her to come over where I'd handed her a drink. She had led me outside, where she'd told me how she was sold by her step-father when her temper became too much for him after her mother died giving birth to his baby. How she was loaded on a ship, raped and beaten during the journey to the States. She admitted she'd attacked and killed one of her captors, gaining her freedom by hiding under a pile of rotting crab for several days. Her temper was one of the things I found attractive in her, a fire I'd once wanted to burn myself in. Now, I wished I could find a way to extinguish it.

"Fine," I snapped, clearing the distance to my bike. "I'll be there in a few. See if you can minimize the damages before Daxx gets wind of it."

Ending the call, I pocketed my phone and straddled my seat. As I secured my helmet, my gaze fell on Emma laughing with a customer as she handed him back his credit card. While I'd known her for a half a second, something told me Emma would never disrespect those who were important to her, a quality I find oddly attractive.

"Fucking hell."

Bullet's voice pulled me from Emma's smile to his concerned face, his gaze however, was captured behind me. Following his line of sight, I found Warden standing outside the club doors, Farrah shoving what looked to be a cellphone into his hand.

"I'd rather have both of my nuts cut off with nail clippers than go see what that is all about."

Judging by the scowl on Warden's face, the conversation couldn't be a good one.

"I'm heading over to Distractions, wanna come along?" I tossed over my shoulder as I kick started my bike.

"Nah, someone needs to be here as a witness in case things with Farrah go south again."

The thump of a deep bass greeted me as I killed the engine and moved the kickstand into place. Distractions was one of the many strip clubs in the downtown area, but the only one owned by a member of the Club.

Several pensive faces lined the entrance, and I could feel their stares as I made my way further into the club. Ignoring the girl dancing on stage, my sights were set on Cisco who was dodging Kira's fists.

"Hey!" I shouted, taking off like a dart across the room. "Quit being a cunt." I seethed, wrapping my arm around her waist and pulling her away from Cisco.

"Put me down, asshole!" She screamed, her kicking feet landing repeatedly on the back of my thigh. "I'm going to kill that fucking bitch."

Slamming my shoulder into the dressing room door, I shoved Kira into the room, my anger escalating as I took in the destruction. Several mirrors were broken, the shattered glass littering the tables and floor.

Chairs laid on their sides, a few with legs broken, their pieces scattered among the fragmented glass.

"Daxx is going to kill you, Kira." I shout, as I rounded on a seething Kira. "What the fuck is all of this?" Gesturing around the room.

This club was Daxx's pride and joy, he'd done me a favor by giving Kira a job in the first place. Once he saw what she'd done, Kira would be lucky if he allowed her to clean the parking lot.

Clearing the distance between us, Kira extended her arm, pointing in the direction of the main room. "They gave my set to that fucking new girl, Lala."

Staring at her through angry eyes, I speared my fingers into the crown of my head, tugging at the strands of hair in an attempt to calm myself.

"I'm the headliner, Hammer. Not some bitch who took a few lessons and wanted a new hobby."

Taking in a deep breath, my gaze dropped to the glass beneath my boots. "You trashed Daxx's club because you didn't get the spot you wanted?"

"Dont you fucking patronize me, Hammer." Emphasizing her words by jamming her finger into my chest. "I've been at this club longer than any of those bitches out there. I've earned this—"

Rage built up inside of my chest, the audacity of her too much to contain. "You've earned nothing, Kira. After all the shit you've done, I had to use my position as VP to get Daxx to let you through the front door."

"No one asked you to." She spat, throwing her arms in the air. "You could have put me in Syn's place, or gone to Kumarin and got my job back at the salon."

Tipping my head back in laughter at the thought of doing any of the things she'd listed. "Let me break things down for you one more time so you understand." Pushing my shoulders back and adjusting my stance, "Even if I went to Kumarin and by some miracle he forgave you for lying to him, your sister would never let you step a single toe over the threshold of her salon."

Years ago, after I'd patched Kira, I rented a space for her to open a salon in downtown Detroit. She'd called her sister, who left a successful business in Chicago to come work with her. Once Kumarin came into the picture, buying the building where the salon was housed and taking over the books, finding out Kira was behind on the rent and hadn't paid her creditors in a while. Once he'd discovered her betrayal, he took the business from her, giving it to her sister who ultimately kicked her out.

"As far as you being a headliner," I scoffed at the idea, for as bad as she was at running a business, she was an even worse dancer. "This is Detroit, not New York or Vegas, nobody comes to a strip club to see five-star entertainment." Leaning further into her space, "Don't think for one second you're anything more than a faceless pussy those bastards picture in their minds as they fuck their wives when they get home."

My bitter words had barely left my lips when Kira's hand connected with my face, the force causing my head to jerk back and a smile to appear on my face.

"You think you're better than me, Hammer?" Kira moved to slap me again, however this time I was ready for her, gripping her wrist before her palm could collide with my face.

"I think you're a psychotic bitch who—"

"Step away from the girl."

Snapping my attention to the doorway, I find a uniformed cop standing there, his gun raised in my direction. His face wasn't familiar, and the slight tremble in his grip didn't escape me.

Drifting my gaze back to Kira's face, it's clear by the smirk on her face she'd fucked him at least once.

"I said, step away from the girl." The cop repeated, his voice laden with borrowed courage.

Locking gazes with Kira, I shoved her wrist away, her triumphant grin like acid on a wound.

"Friend of yours?" I nodded my head toward the cop, causing her smirk to intensify.

"Not every man is a Neanderthal jerk."

"Neanderthal?" I huffed. "Since when did you start swallowing dictionaries instead of cum?"

"Keep your hands where I can see them." The cop demanded, either oblivious to our banter, or too lost in his assumption of how this would play out to notice our quarrel was over before it began.

"Calm the fuck down, Barney." I began, but as I turned to give this rookie motherfucker a piece of my mind, he slammed into me, shoving me across the room and against the wall.

"You like hitting on ladies half your size?" A smile formed on my lips as the sound of handcuffs closing filled the air. I could smell the adrenaline pumping through his veins, and I imagine he truly believed he was the hero, coming to save the damsel in distress.

"Two things wrong with your assumption," I began as he attempted to jerk me off the wall. I outweighed him by at least sixty pounds, and have him by several inches. "One, Kira has never been a lady a day in her life." Pushing myself off the wall, I allowed him to turn me around, dropping my gaze to the sweat beading on his upper lip. " Two, the only time I've ever laid a hand on that bitch, was when she'd begged me to spank her while I fucked her."

Rage flickered in the officer's eyes at my statement, gaining me the opportunity to lower my eyes to the nameplate on his uniform. *'Johnson'*, I repeated internally, pinning it to memory.

"You're under arrest for domestic violence, Asshole." Johnson spat, hooking his hand on my arm and jerking me toward the door.

Planting my feet firmly on the floor, I cast a hard look in Kira's direction. Hairs on the back of my neck stood at attention, an internal warning about this being an elaborate setup. "You sure this is how you want to play this?"

Kira remained silent, her once victorious smile now a well-practiced scowl.

"Okay, darlin', but just remember, you're the one who laid down the gauntlet, not me."

Johnson tugged at my arm. "You have the right to remain silent," he began. "I suggest you exercise it."

Tossing my head back, I let out a laugh as he pulled me through the club, passing several of my brothers and the newest dancer on stage, who I assumed was the one to get Kira's feathers ruffled. The redhead had curves in all the right places, the mask covering her face gave her an air of mystery, something no doubt Kira was pissed she hadn't thought of first.

"I'll call Kannon, Hammer. We'll have you out in an hour," Keys shouted as Johnson tried to shove my shoulder to get me moving faster.

"Don't bother, man, the whole thing is bullshit. Officer Johnson here got his dick sucked by a seasoned whore and now he thinks he's in love. Too bad for him, Kira is incapable of loving anything, including herself." The latter was spoken as we hit the door, my gaze firmly locked with Kira's

Emma

CHAPTER
SEVEN

EMMA

THE NUMBERS on the page began to blur. Blinking my eyes, I shook my head and reached for the mug of coffee on my desk. My body was running on fumes as my sleep had been interrupted by a drunken phone call from Macy just after midnight. She'd screamed and cussed when I'd declined her repeated demands for money. However, it was her threat I would never see my nephew again which kept me awake after she'd hung up the phone, sending all of my repeated calls to voicemail.

Having the choice between tossing and turning the remainder of the night, or getting a head start on sorting through old invoices, the numbers game won out.

It'd become evident, somewhere around the time the sun came up, Syn's desk wasn't the only thing a complete mess in this office.

"Excuse me, beautiful?" A deep voice called from across the room. The intensity of it woke me up much better than the two pots of coffee sitting like a hot stone in my stomach. "I'm here to pick up my car."

Snapping my attention in the direction of the door, the intensity of the voice was reflected in the suited man standing in the doorway.

"I didn't mean to startle you." A smile curled the edge of his lips as he took several steps to separate the distance between us. "I'm Nick, and you are?"

My mouth ran dry as I stared at his outstretched hand, the sun reflecting off the metal of the Rolex peeking out of his jacket sleeve.

"Audi," I stupidly said, a direct reaction to the silkiness of his voice. "I m-mean…" Stuttering, I dropped his hand and turned back to my computer. "You're the owner of the Audi. Mr. Havarov?"

Drawing in a cleansing breath, I snapped my gaze back to the rich eyes of the man before me. "I see you've paid online, thank you for that. Would you like a printed receipt?"

"What I'd like," Nick began, the smoothness of his voice intensifying. "Is to know your name."

I knew who he was, more importantly who he's connected to. My time here was temporary, and I considered giving him a fictitious name. However, as I opened my mouth to spew the lie, the door to the shop opened.

"Emma, I need a favor from you." Layla stepped into the room, her phone in hand and a determined look on her face. She stopped short, "Oh, hello, Nick." Her shocked eyes morphed into a more appreciative stare.

I couldn't blame Layla, Nick was an extremely attractive man, composed of equal parts charisma and cunning. His reputation as one of the deadliest men alive, however, kept my tongue silent as to my identity.

"Layla," his tone was so smooth it made you want to coat your skin in it. "Always a pleasure." Reaching out, Nick ran his fingers along Layla's arm as he exited the room, allowing me to set free the breath I'd held since he'd walked in.

"You said you needed a favor."

Layla slowly turned to face me, rubbing the area of her arm where Nick had touched her. "Yeah," she spoke breathlessly, clearly her mind still lingering on the interaction.

"There's a party tomorrow night, we're telling certain people it's a welcome to the club thing for you."

Tilting my head to the side in confusion, I moved to open my mouth to question her when she raised her hand to stop me.

"Just do me a favor. If Jillian asks you about it, I need you to tell her Warden offered and you don't want to piss him off."

"Piss who off?"

My gaze snapped to the man in question standing inside the door, his usually intense face, softened in confusion. Warden has grown on me in the last few days, his once intimidating gruffness now a welcomed characteristic. I knew where I stood with him, something I couldn't say about many people.

"You, dumbass," Layla tossed over her shoulder. "I'm filling Emma in on the plans for tomorrow night."

Warning flags were flapping in the proverbial breeze as I took in the silent exchanges between the pair.

"Did you at least tell her what's happening?"

"Yes."

"No."

Layla and I spoke simultaneously.

Hooking his hands on his hips, Warden shook his head, "Of course you didn't." He grumbled as he turned toward me. "Emma, I need you to blindly follow us on this. If anyone asks, tell them the party is for you. I need you to show up long enough for Bullet to do his thing and then you can cut out and go home."

I thought for the briefest of moments to probe further, demanding to know what was happening at this party.

"Have you seen Hammer today?" I questioned instead, tapping the file on my desk. "I need his signature on these checks."

It's been my experience, the less you say speaks louder than shouting at the top of your lungs.

Dropping his gaze to the file, Warden rounded the desk as Layla silently waved goodbye and left the room.

"Hammer's in jail."

"Oh," I'm caught off guard. "T-that would make signing these checks hard, wouldn't it?" A nervous laugh left my throat as Warden reached for a pen from the cup on my desk.

"They're bullshit charges. Kira and her new fuck buddy trying to flex muscle they don't have."

I tried not to ponder what he meant, instead focusing on his hand as he scribed a surprisingly elegant signature on each check.

"We'll get you on the account first thing." He finished, returning the pen to the cup before standing to his full height. "I appreciate your coop-eration with the party, it means a lot to Bullet."

A clap of thunder rattled the windows, forcing a gasp from my throat and robbing me of the opportunity to remind Warden I had no idea who this Bullet was. Turning to the stack of bills,

"You poor motherfucker." Warden laughed, pulling my attention from the much overdue invoices to the man atop a motorcycle pulling into the lot, the torrential downpour soaking him to the bone.

I watched as the man parked the bike as if the blinding rain was no more than a spring breeze. It wasn't until the man stood from the bike, pulling the helmet off and tossing it to the ground below that I realized it's not some stranger, but Hammer.

"He'll need something hot," I mumbled, moving around Warden and heading for the coffee pot. Reaching for the first mug I came to, I was about to fill it with coffee when Hammer walked through the door, tugging his wet T-shirt over the top of his head. My breath hitched as I took in the defined muscles of his naked chest. My tongue peaked out to wet my lips as I read Liam's name tattooed vertically on his ribs.

"You okay, brother?"

The sound of Warden's voice pulled me from my lust-filled haze, steering my focus back to the mug in my hand.

"Never fucking better," Hammer clipped, the sharpness in his tone sending a chill down my spine. Warden's story of where Hammer spent the day pushed to the forefront of my mind, reminding me to fill the cup. Internally chastising myself for lusting after my boss, I wrapped my fingers around the handle of the mug. "Here, Hammer, this should warm you up."

Keeping my focus on the black liquid inside the mug, I extended my hand out to him.

"Thanks, darlin'."

His term of endearment caused a smile to form on my face, but it's the sensation running up my arm when his fingers brush mine, which forces my gaze to snap to his.

Hammer seemed unaffected as he took the cup from my hand, sending me a wink as he brought the mug to his lips.

"You're welcome," I offered, reaching out to take his wet shirt. "I'll go find you something to dry off with."

My mind flashed to the linen closet I'd stumbled across when searching for the bathroom. Cisco had found me flustered in the hall, giving me a tour of the back rooms which included a decent sized kitchen and the door which led to the private rooms the members of the Club used for whatever. Like the door across the parking lot, he cautioned me not to venture inside the black door.

"That's not necessary, darlin'."

Hammer's fingers gripped the thick part of my arm, halting my progression. "No amount of Michigan rain will ever get rid of county jail stench. I need a hot shower and something a little stiffer to drink."

Smiling shyly, I nodded before moving to round my desk, the skin of my arm tingling from his touch.

"Make it quick, Hammer. I need you to take Emma to the bank and put her on the accounts."

Warden's words held authority, forcing my gaze to the profile of his left side and the pair of hot pink lips tattooed on his neck.

"Sure," Hammer nodded. "Give me five minutes to shower and we can go."

Opening my mouth to answer him, the words were halted by Warden's banter. "Don't bullshit our girl. You know it's going to take five minutes to find your minuscule dick."

Raising his cup into the air, "You really have to stop assuming everyone has the same tiny dick as you." Sending me a wink, Hammer disappeared down the hall.

Rain drops pounded the windshield, the blinding sheets making it difficult for the wipers to keep up.

"How long have you lived in Michigan?"

"Just over four years."

Hammer's question surprised me as I'd assumed he'd read my resumé. Then again, Roxie made it a point of letting me know the Club had chosen me based on my lack of association with any of the members.

"So you moved here for college then?"

"Michigan offered me the most for my buck, so it was an easy choice." It wasn't a complete lie, the University of Michigan had offered me a sizable scholarship, yet nothing close to the one Ohio State tried to tempt me with. Distance had been the deciding factor in my choice to attend college here.

"What about you, have you always lived here?"

Hammer slowed the car before glancing over his shoulder to check the traffic from our left. "I was born in Florida. My parents met when my dad was attending Bike Week in Daytona. Mom turned eighteen a week after I was born, boarded a bus and called my father when she made it to Detroit. He took one look at me and moved us in with him. My sister was born a few years later."

Letting out a silent breath, I dropped my gaze to my hands resting in my lap. "Sounds like a storybook romance," I deadpanned, jealousy wrapped around each word.

"Storybook?" Hammer scoffed, steering the car as if the rain didn't affect him. "Hardly. My parents fought like hell, especially when it came to Club business."

Nodding his head toward me. "Wait for me inside. I'll park the car and be right behind you."

Snapping my gaze to the building beside us, the implication of what he's suggesting hitting me. "This is completely unnecessary, I can walk—."

My pleading was cut off by the soft touch of his fingers against my cheek. "Humor me, Emma, my father taught me respect above all else. In my position in the Club, my role as a provider for my son, and in keeping a beautiful lady out of the rain."

The combination of his touch and closeness left me unable to argue.

Nodding my head, I pulled away from his touch, jerking the door open and running toward the entrance.

Once inside, I was greeted by the chilled temperature of the air conditioned room.

"Hello, can we help you?"

Donning my best smile, I reached up to wipe away a wayward drop of water. Taking a step forward, "Yes, I'm here—"

"We're here to see Craig Sheppard." Hammer caused me to gasp with his sudden appearance.

"Do you have an appointment, Mr…" The woman behind the desk drifted off, waiting for Hammer to fill in the blank.

"Trust me, darlin', I don't need one."

Just as his touch was disarming to me, the smoothness and confidence in his voice had the woman before us melting at his words.

"Tell him Jonathan is here to see him."

The woman nodded before picking up the phone, whispering into the mouthpiece while keeping her eyes trained on Hammer.

"Mr. Sheppard will see you now, I'm told you already know the way."

Hammer gripped my hand, "That I do, darlin'." He bade the woman as he lead me around the small desk and toward a closed door at the back of the room.

"Jonathan?" I whispered in bewilderment.

"My mother was alone when I was born, named me after her grandfather who'd passed away the year before."

"Then why do they call you Hammer?" The question was out of my mouth of its own volition. "I'm sorry—" I began, regretting the intrusion immediately.

"That's a story for another day, Emma." Sending me a wink, Hammer rapped his knuckles on the wooden door. "Let's get this over with first."

Nodding, I shared a smile with him as a deep voice on the other side beckoned us in. As we passed over the threshold, I noticed the nameplate on the door, *Craig Sheppard, President*.

"Tell me you're not here to close your accounts?" The tall man standing behind the simple desk questioned as he rounded the corner to embrace Hammer in a back-slapping hug. As the pair exchanged greetings, I took in the similarities between them. Craig was an older, yet still handsome version of Hammer, giving me the assumption this was either his father or a close relative.

"Not yet, Uncle, you still have the best return rates in the city." Squeezing my hand, Hammer pulled me closer. "I'm here to add Emma to the Club accounts."

"Oh?" Craig looked at me with inquisitive eyes, his uncomfortable survey sending a chill up my spine. "I wasn't aware you'd fired Synthia."

"Syn's doctors have put her on bedrest. Emma is handling our affairs until the baby is born."

"Pregnant? Is there a chance—?" Craig didn't need to elaborate, I'd heard the story of how Syn had been intimate with nearly every member of the Club.

Hammer let out a heavy sigh, his free hand combing through the hair atop his head. "We've arranged to have a paternity test as soon as the baby is born."

"I see." Craig lowered his gaze, nodding his head as he rounded his desk and returned to his seat. "You'll have to excuse me, Emma. I leave these particular tasks to my employees out front. However, considering the sensitive nature of my nephew's occupation..."

"It's fine," I offered in hopes of changing the subject. "This isn't my first time performing this type of banking transaction."

"Worked as a bank teller, have we?" Craig's voice was laced with condescension I couldn't fault him for. I have zero doubt he was used to dealing with women like Syn and Roxie.

"No, sir, I'm a Forensic Accountant."

Craig leaned back in his seat, the color draining from his face. "Forensic Accountant?" His eyes snapping to Hammer standing beside me. "Why in the hell do you need one of those?"

Placing my hand on the desk, "Mr. Sheppard, if I may? The relationship Hammer and I have is serendipitous. He needed a temporary assistant and I needed a job to tide me over until my credentialing process was complete. Both of which will come to a close once Syn gives birth in a few months."

I could see the disbelief written on the fine details of Craig's face. I'd dealt with men like him for the majority of my life, willing to bend a few rules as long as it benefited their bottom line.

"I think it would be best if we kept my access limited to the accounts for the towing company. An activity tracker with the minimum—"

"Give her all access, Uncle. And a debit card for the Club account." Hammer interrupted, tossing his body into the closest chair. "She's done more for us in three days than Syn did in all the years she's collected a paycheck."

Hammer

CHAPTER
EIGHT
HAMMER

"YOU'RE SO FUCKING BEAUTIFUL." I whispered against porcelain skin, grinding my hard cock into the delicate flesh of a female backside, kneading a heavy breast in the palm of my hand.

"I want you so bad," she begged, arching her back as she reached her tiny hand between us and grasped my cock.

"Then take me, baby," I demanded as I flipped onto my back, bringing the giggling girl with me.

Placing my hands behind my head, I closed my eyes as I felt her straddle me, running the head of my cock between her slick lips.

"Hammer?" Her sweet voice called, her fingers brushing against my sensitive balls.

"Yes, Emma," I moved my hands to her hips, struggling to open my eyes.

"Hammer," her voice was muffled as if she were underwater, causing my heart to race as my eyes refused to open.

"Hammer, wake up, man." The once delicate voice is now deep with testosterone, forcing my eyes open and jerking me straight up in bed.

"What the fuck?" Scanning the room, my heart hammering in my ears as I reached for my gun tucked under my pillow, pointing it at the end of my bed.

"It's me, you lazy bastard," Warden cautioned, the light from the hall illuminating his massive stature. "Get dressed, motherfucker. I need to talk with you."

Tossing my gun to the mattress beside me, my cock still hard and tenting the sheets around my hips. This was the second night I'd dreamed of fucking Emma. I'd blame the dreams on eating dinner too late, but that would have been a lie, and I'm sick of being lied to. Between catching her checking out my naked chest and being surrounded by the scent of her floral perfume, I'd been rock hard since she'd arrived in the office.

"What fucking time is it?" I mumbled as I picked up my phone to discover it's just after three in the morning.

"Time for you get the fuck out of bed so I can talk with you." Warden called from down the hall, the volume of his voice making me pause and listen for Liam.

When all I heard was the hiss of his humidifier, I swung my legs over the side of my bed, sliding my feet into my discarded pants and tugging them over my hips.

Joining Warden in my living room, "Keep your voice down, Warden. You wake Liam and I will kick your ass."

Nodding, Warden leaned back into the leather of my couch. "How's he doing?" Nodding his head in the direction of Liam's room.

Dropping my tired body onto the chair across from him, "He's been at Kira's for the last few days."

Liam was born with a rare form of asthma, one so vicious it doesn't take much to send him into an attack. I'd made adjustments in the house, installing commercial grade air filters and had the house professionally cleaned to help keep his attacks at bay. Kira on the other hand, refused to follow the doctor's orders, claiming Liam needed to be exposed to as many germs as possible to harden his immune system. Calling specialists, including Doc Ash, crazy for insisting his disease had nothing to do with a weak immune system.

"So he's headed for an emergency room visit?"

Rubbing my hands over my face, "Hopefully not. He's spent more time with Mrs. Flowers than he has with Kira."

I'd lost count of how many times we'd rushed Liam to the emergency room, watching as his doctor pumped gallons of medications into him to help him breathe.

"That's good." Warden nodded, his attention seeming to be a million miles away.

Unease began stirring inside my chest. None of my Club brothers made it a habit of dropping by after midnight, especially Warden.

"Did something happen today while I was at the bank?"

Leaning his arms over his thighs, Warden dropped his attention to his boots before spearing his fingers into his hair, combing back the strands as his gaze snapped to mine.

"What I'm about to tell you stays in the room, feel me?"

Nodding, I mimicked his stance.

"I got word earlier this evening, Ace McKenzie is looking to retire, and he's tossed my name around as a possible replacement."

Ace was the SOC National Chapter President. Having held the position for as long as I could recall.

"Fuck." I swore, tossing my back into the cushion of the chair. My mind flooded with what this would mean to the Club.

Warden rubbed his hands on his thighs, his face turning pensive. "I got a call earlier, saying to expect a visit from Ace tonight."

"Are you serious? What about Bullet, this is—"

"Bullet knows Club business comes before anything else." Warden cut me off, his voice laced with venom.

"Are you considering taking the position?"

"Depends," Warden let the single word hang in the air between us as he studied my face. "Do you see yourself taking my place as chapter president?"

A heaviness fell over the table as Warden called Church to order. Bullet sat with his leg bouncing a mile a minute, while Kannon spoke in hushed tones into his cell phone.

"Before we get to Club business, you need to know Farrah has bent the knee and apologized to Erin."

I struggled to keep the scowl off my face, having heard about Farrah's lackluster apology. According to Roxie, Farrah showed up at the diner while the girls were having lunch with Emma, demanded to speak with Erin and then tossed out a, "My bad", before spinning on her heels and jumping into the car with her detective boyfriend.

"I've spoken with Erin, who assured me she has accepted the apology and holds no ill-feelings toward my wife."

I held my tongue as I searched the faces around the table, knowing they all knew this apology of Farrah's was as fake as her tits.

"Erin's a goddamn saint," Raiden tossed, leaning back in his chair. "Not a mean bone in her fucking body."

"Unless you're fucking her," Daxx added, earning a slap to the back of his head from Raiden and a chorus of snickers from the table.

Tuning out Raiden and Daxx's banter, I perused the faces of the men surrounding the table, every eye trained on Warden. Would my brothers accept me as president? Did I even want the role?

"Bad news, fuckers." Kannon's raised voice shattered my insecurities. "Boom made bail before my guy could get to him."

A murmur of oaths filled the table as Kannon pocketed his phone and took his seat at the table.

"Who?" Warden demanded, the valley between his brows deepening and he slipped deeper into his leather chair.

"According to the bail bonds it was a woman by the name of Iryish Huntley."

Shifting my gaze to Chopper, "Name ringing any bells?"

"There's more," Kannon added before Chopper could take a breath to answer.

"Hailey used her contacts to find the address for Ms. Huntley. When my guy showed up, he found her apartment trashed, a broken cell phone beside a purse with her wallet and ID still inside."

Snapping my gaze back to Chopper. "What do you know about this Iryish?"

Chopper shrugged, "Never heard of her, and I'd remember a name like Iryish."

Keeping my focus on Chopper, I'm not convinced he's telling the truth. "Kannon, ask Hailey to do some more digging, find out all she can about this Iryish chick." I had a feeling wherever this girl was, Boon would be too.

"Already working on it, Hammer." Kannon assured, tapping his fingers against the table. I could see it in his eyes, he had doubts about Chopper too.

Emma

CHAPTER
NINE

EMMA

I'D SWORN to Layla I would hang around the party until Bullet proposed to Jillian, a ruse to make her believe this party was for me and not her.

"Here you go, darlin'." A red cup appeared in front of me, Chopper's bright smile shining down on me.

"Thanks," I offered, taking the cup from his fingers, with no real intention of drinking the chilled concoction inside. I'd attended enough fraternity parties to know better than to consume a drink I didn't ask for.

The parking lot outside my office had been transformed from a well-used paved piece of land, to something resembling a backyard barbecue. Café lights were strung from the Clubhouse to the top of the garage bay, their lights joining forces with a number of firepits to illuminate the space while keeping it rustic. Several picnic tables had been set up this afternoon, anchored under large tents erected under Layla's watchful eye. A catering van arrived not long after the last tent was complete, the two men inside built a fire in each of the massive smokers, the smell of cooking meat making my stomach grumble.

"Here," a soft voice to my left preceded the feel of something cold against my left arm. "Drink this instead."

Glancing to my left, I find Hailey's bruised face smiling back at me, a can of soda in her outstretched hand.

"How's the face?" I asked, tossing the contents of the red cup to the ground, slipping the closed can of soda in its place.

"Not as bad as I worried it would be. We'll see if I say the same in five weeks." She snickered, raising her matching can of soda in my direction as a toast. Hailey was due for her second oral surgery in a little over a month.

"Oh dear lord."

Tilting my head to the side, I stared at her through confused eyes. "Excuse me?"

Hailey shifted her gaze to something over my right shoulder, her face contorting in disbelief. Turning my head, I followed her line of sight just in time to see a man standing on one of the picnic tables, a bottle to his lips. My breath caught as he dropped the bottle, the glass shattering on the pavement before a ball of fire shot from his mouth.

"What's up, fuckers?" He shouted, the crowd gathering around going wild with cheers. "You ready to party?" The crowd's response was even louder this time.

"Who is that?" The question was out of my mouth of its own volition.

"That, my friend," Hailey moved closer to me, pointing her index finger in the man's direction. "Is Daxx Inman, Sergeant at Arms for the Club."

So this was the infamous Daxx I'd heard of, the unachievable man Roxie so desperately wanted. I could see the appeal. He was a handsome man with his dark hair and tan skin, the smattering of facial hair giving him an edge.

"What kind of road name is Daxx?"

"Trust me, if Daxx had a road name it would be Man Whore." Hailey huffed, popping the top of her can of soda.

"Aren't all bikers?" It was rhetorical, however as I looked into Hailey's eyes I regretted the comment immediately.

"Touché," Hailey nodded, tapping her soda can to my own.

"I'm sorry—"

"You know, your slip of the tongue got me thinking the other day."

Hailey interrupted, wrapping her arm around mine and moving us forward. My heart hovered somewhere in my throat as Hailey led me toward the fence which surrounded the lot. "So, I did some digging."

Remaining silent, I smiled at several of the men we passed.

"Emma Diane Shaw, daughter of Darrin and Sherry Shaw and sister to Macy. Your family lived in Alabama until your father accepted a job in Kentucky with the railroad. Three years later, he was involved in an unfortunate accident which rendered him unable to return to work."

Memories of the day I'd watched my mother drop to her knees when men from my father's company came to tell her of the accident flooded my mind. I was thirteen when my dad came home and announced we were moving to Kentucky, promising us life would be easier. We'd packed our meager belongings into the back of our minivan, the thing breaking down three times before we made it to Kentucky. Our life wasn't any easier as my father called out of work more than he showed up. My mother eventually grew tired of his excuses, threatening to pack us up and leave if he didn't go to work.

"Workers' Comp deemed the railroad liable for the accident and your father was given a sizable compensation check, which your mother used to open a bar."

An involuntary laugh left my throat at the mention of my mother's bar. Her joy of giving us the life my father had promised was stolen by his lies.

"Did your investigation tell you the accident also left my father addicted to opioids? Or how they found him dead in the back of our van from an overdose?"

Hailey's eyes grew wide as she stopped our progression. "I-I," she stuttered. However, the anger was brewing in my chest at the audacity of her diving into my personal life and fueled my verbal assault.

"Did you go running to Kannon when you learned how he'd left us over a hundred-thousand dollars in debt? Did he give you an attaboy when you told him how my mother lost ownership of the bar to the man who'd sold him drugs when his doctor stopped prescribing them?"

Tears sprang to my eyes at the memory of my mother's face as she'd sat in the bar, sobbing as the mountain of a man shoved paperwork in front of her, signing over majority ownership to him.

"I swear, I didn't go that far," Hailey shouted, grabbing me by the shoulders and pulling me into a tight hug. "When you'd mentioned property patching, I had to make sure you weren't a plant from another Club." She whispered in my ear, her voice cracking with emotion

Pushing out of her embrace, "Did you find what you were looking for?"

Hailey wiped a tear from her eye, shaking her head. "Just your sister's criminal record. Which has nothing to do with you, I know."

Taking two measured steps back, Hailey matched each footfall. "Listen, I apologize for going behind your back, but not for trying to protect my family. Kannon and I may not be what he wants us to be, but I owe him, and this Club, my life."

Seeing the truth reflecting in Hailey's eyes, I stopped my backward progression. "How did they save you?"

Hailey shook her head, dropping her gaze to the concrete below her feet. The memory of the cryptic conversation between her and Roxie sprang to mind.

"It's fine, Hailey. Unlike you, I will respect your right to privacy."

Spinning on my heels, I caught Bullet pulling a red faced Jillian to the center of the parking lot. The smile on her face was almost enough to chase the scowl off mine. I watched with longing as he confessed how much he loved and adored her, how a lifetime with her wouldn't be enough. A pang of jealousy slashed at my heart when he dropped to one knee and asked her to spend forever with him. I clapped along with everyone else when Jillian gave him a tearful yes. When he picked her up bridal style and crossed the lot, I tossed my drink into a nearby trash can and headed toward my car. I'd kept my word to Layla and now it was time to go home.

Glancing in the rearview mirror, I caught sight of Hailey still standing where I'd left her. I hated the sadness in her eyes, but as I moved to shut off the car, my phone rang a familiar tune. Sucking in a deep breath, I smashed the button on my steering wheel.

"What do you want, Clark?"

Hammer

CHAPTER
TEN

HAMMER

"YOUR SISTER DID GOOD, BROTHER."

Nodding my head in agreement, I tapped my beer against Kannon's before raising it to my lips and taking a healthy pull.

"She gave Bullet her word he wouldn't be disappointed."

Gripping the bottle in my hand, I bounced back and forth on the balls of my feet as I searched the lot for Emma. I'd hoped to arrive at the party earlier, but Kira made it impossible. Tonight was her night to have Liam, and as per usual, she'd had a million things which needed my attention.

"She left about five minutes ago."

Snapping my attention to Kannon, staring at him through confused eyes. "Who?"

Kannon shook his head, a knowing smile splitting his face. "Emma," he chuckled as he spoke her name. "Don't worry, Hammer." He leaned in as if to whisper, "Your secret is safe with me."

Spinning in his direction, I moved mere inches from him. "What the fuck are you talking about? What secret?"

My raised voice gained the attention of a few Club chicks, however I couldn't give a shit.

"Listen, brother," Kannon stepped closer, our noses within a hair-width apart. "This Club pays me a lot of money for my attention to detail, my ability to dig up forgotten facts, and most importantly, my loyalty. I've watched you around her. Listened as you've spoken her name as if a prayer in the wind. Now, maybe you're looking to fuck her, but my gut tells me you want the same thing from Emma that I want from Hailey."

Opening my mouth to tell him to fuck off and mind his own business, my retort was halted by a frail voice.

"I didn't mean to do it."

Snapping my attention to a tearful Hailey.

"Do what, Baby?" Our argument forgotten as Kannon bent at the knees to bring himself to her height, gripping her shoulders in a protective stance.

Hailey snapped her gaze to me, keeping her hands gripped tightly on Kannon's shoulders. Those baby blues full of remorse.

"The other day, at lunch, Emma said..." She trailed off, the sobs stealing her breath.

Looking at Kannon, I tipped my head toward the garage bay behind us, silently telling him we needed to move this conversation to a more private location.

"It's okay, sweetheart. I'm sure we can fix whatever it is." Kannon assured, pulling Hailey into his protective embrace.

Once inside the bay, I hopped onto one of the cabinets as Kannon pulled a stool out for Hailey.

"All right, sweetheart, tell us what's wrong."

Giving the pair a moment, I cast my attention to my boots as they swayed back and forth. As much as I hated to admit it, Kannon had been correct in his assumption on my interest in Emma. Did I want to fuck her? Hell yes I did. Was that all I wanted? I hadn't decided yet.

"Emma said something the other day, I'd assumed it was a slip of the tongue." Hailey tipped her head back, her eyes cast to the ceiling.

"What did she say?" I prodded when she'd been silent for too long.

"She said she had no interest in being 'property patched'."

Hailey took a deep breath and continued with her version of the conversation which had transpired at the diner and of the extensive background check she'd done on Emma. This wasn't the first time I'd heard what Emma had said. Roxie called me not two minutes after she'd left the diner.

"I am so sorry, Hammer. I know how hard you searched for someone to fill in for Syn and now you may lose her because of me."

Pushing myself off the cabinet, I took several steps to clear the distance between Hailey and myself. Bending down, I palmed her face.

"Emma doesn't strike me as the kind of girl who'd hold a grudge."

"But I violated her trust by searching her history out of curiosity." Hailey argued back, remorse coating her emotional words.

Nodding, I dropped my hands to hers, squeezing her shaking fingers. "I seem to recall a beautiful girl who held a loaded shotgun to one of my brothers when he'd gotten too close to her business."

I'll never forget the look on Bullet's face when he'd come around the corner of Hailey's trailer, his hands raised in the air with Hailey trailing behind, a shotgun pointed at his back.

"Please don't remind me," she smiled through her tears. "Bullet still calls me Gun Toting Hailey."

"He's right, love," Kannon placed a kiss on the top of her head. "You apologized to Bullet, and tomorrow, after everyone involved has had time to decompress, you'll come in and do the same with Emma."

Standing to my full height, I was half-tempted to tell Hailey what she'd discovered about Emma's past wasn't a tenth of what I'd been able to uncover.

Stepping from the shower, I wrapped a towel around my waist, bracing my arms against the counter and listened to the stillness in the house. I'd driven to Emma's apartment after leaving the party, worried she had, as Hailey assumed, decided to quit. I'd sat on my bike for over an hour, watching her through an open window, unable to pull my eyes away from her as she sat behind her laptop. I imagined myself approaching her from behind, closing the laptop and laying her across the table, filling her over and over.

"Maybe all I do want is to fuck her," I deadpanned to my reflection in the mirror, my inner voice screaming I was a goddamn liar.

The sound of my doorbell put an end to any battle plans I'd need to formulate, if and when I chose to pursue Emma. Checking the time on my microwave, I reached for my gun as whoever was standing on the other side of the door pushed the button again.

Checking the side window, I blew out a breath when I saw Roxie standing on my front porch, her hand raised to push the button once more. Taking wide steps to the front door, I twisted the locks, wrenching the door open.

"What?" I demanded, a little louder than I'd intended. Roxie stood with her bottom lip trapped between her teeth, her gaze locked on my naked chest.

"If I didn't know better, I would think you were expecting me." Reaching out, Roxie ran her polished fingernail down the center of my chest.

"Cut the shit, Roxie. What do you want?"

Her gaze cut to mine, the hunger there making my cock twitch.

"I want to suck your cock dry, Hammer." She admitted, shoving my chest with her open hands, forcing me to take several steps back to keep from falling.

Everyone, especially Daxx, knew she had it bad for him. Yet, she wasn't stupid enough to sit around and wait for him to have some sort of epiphany before making her his. She used each of us as much as we used her, and while she wasn't as kinky as Kira, she definitely knew how to suck a motherfucker dry.

"You won't be needing this," she whispered, jerking the edge of my towel and falling to her knees, taking the terrycloth with her.

Dropping back my head, a hiss left my mouth with the first stroke of her tongue along the underside of my shaft. Warmth, like a blanket fresh out of the dryer, enveloped me. The hum from her throat had me reaching down and gripping her hair in my fist.

"Fuck," I swore as she wrapped a hand around my shaft, drawing me in and out of her mouth at a rapid pace.

My mind flashed back to Emma as she sat at her kitchen table, the fantasy I'd imagined coming to life.

"That's it, baby," I encouraged, slipping the head closer to the back of her throat as she tugged on my balls.

"Fuck yes, Emma," I chanted, realizing my mistake when Roxie hesitated, but continued, putting everything she had into getting me off. Seconds later, my orgasm hit like a freight train, stealing my breath and leaving me feeling guilty. Reaching down, I grabbed my towel, offering it to Roxie who wiped the corner of her mouth.

"Thanks, Hammer. For the…you know, and for this." She raised the towel before handing it back to me.

Without ceremony, she spun on her heels and headed for the door. Pausing, Roxie looked over her shoulder. "Oh, and Hammer? There's something about Emma you should know, before you decide to fuck her."

Emma

CHAPTER
ELEVEN

EMMA

"HEY, DO YOU HAVE A MINUTE?"

Shifting my attention from the email on my screen to Hailey standing inside my office door.

"Of course." I smiled, waving her inside.

Shaking her head, Hailey crossed the room, tucking her navy skirt before sitting fluidly into a chair.

"I come bearing gifts." Digging into her bag, Hailey pulled out a plastic container, popping the lid before showing me the contents. "I may suck at being a good friend, but I make a mean dessert bar."

Tilting my head to the side, I shared a sad smile. "This is completely unnecessary," I admitted, reaching for a corner piece. "I spoke with a good friend last night who said I should be accustomed to extensive background checks."

"The IRS, right?" Hailey confirmed, closing the lid and sitting the container on my desk.

"Hopefully," I admitted, the email she interrupted was a request for more information.

"I've seen your credentials, trust me, you have nothing to worry about." Her eyes grew wide as Hailey covered her mouth.

"My grandmother would get out of her grave and beat me if she could hear how rude I've been."

Raising my cookie in the air. "Here's to starting over."

Hailey placed her hands together as if in prayer. "Thank you, Emma. I acted horribly, and I want to make it up to you. Since I know so much about you, I feel it's only fair you know about me."

Shaking my head, Hailey held her hand up to me, then proceeded to tell me the story of a man who'd used her and treated her badly.

"Want to know why I haven't jumped into a relationship with Kannon? Because for as long as I can recall, I've been told how ugly I am. I've made the mistake of falling for men like Kannon, and never, not once, did it work out in my favor."

Reaching across the desk, I laid my hand on Hailey's arm. "I know people can be cruel, however, you know it's not fair to judge one man based on the sins of another."

Hailey nodded, her eyes downcast. "I do, and trust me, I wish I could toss caution to the wind and let him in. He is the single most amazing man I've ever met..." Hailey trailed off, her voice coated with raw emotion.

"Tell me; if today were Kannon's last day on earth, would you regret not giving him a chance?"

I watched as something flashed in Hailey's eyes, as if my word registered deep within her soul.

"You're smart to keep your distance, Hailey." A gasp left my throat as I turned my attention to Farrah who stood inside the door, staring at the pair of us. "Kannon may be a talented attorney, but he's an SOC at heart. A faithful biker is an exclusion, not the rule. Best to leave men like him to women who are used to riding on the wild side."

Her voice was laced with venom, with as many harsh edges as the severe makeup she wore.

"And on that note, I have things to do." Standing to her full height, Hailey rounded the corner of my desk, wrapped me in a side hug. "Thanks for the advice, Emma," she whispered before placing a kiss to my cheek. I watched as Hailey walked passed Farrah without a word of acknowledgement.

"Is there something I can help you with?" I needed to get Farrah out of my office before she contaminated the space with her negativity.

"Syn sent me over to pick up her money."

Shifting my attention to my computer screen, "You're a day too late. I mailed her paycheck yesterday."

"Paycheck?" Farrah scoffed as if the word left a bad taste in her mouth. "Since when does SOC leave paper trails?"

"I'm sorry." Turning my head in her direction, narrowing my eyes as the audacity of her is astounding. "I don't think it's appropriate to discuss business with you."

"Need I remind you I'm married to Warden?"

I had to bite the inside of my lips to keep from laughing. I'd heard the guys in the shop talk about the tumultuous relationship between Warden and Farrah.

"Need I remind you if Warden wanted you involved in his business, he wouldn't have hired me."

Farrah's face shifted from her perfected bitch face, to one much more severe. Had I not dealt with Macy all my life, Farrah may have intimidated me.

"Don't—"

Raising my index finger toward her, the ringing of my phone interrupting what I suspect would have been a colorful retort.

"SOC Automotive?" I answered in my sticky-sweet voice, an eyebrow raised in challenge at Farrah.

"Hello, may I please speak with Mr. Jonathan Sheppard?"

The way the man on the other side of the line spoke Hammer's given name left a chill down my spine.

"May I say who is calling?"

My gut filled with dread as the man identified himself. I was on my feet, running as fast as I could across the lot as he told me of the urgency of his call.

"Hold on, sir. I'm almost there." I panted into the receiver as the forbidden door grew closer. Knowing the punishment for defying Warden's rules, I twisted the handle, slamming my shoulder into the metal door.

"Hammer!" I shout, covering the receiver with my hand to protect the hearing of the man on the other side. Two men demanded for me to stop as I ran by a long bar on my left. Searching the room, I noticed a closed set of double doors with the SOC logo carved into the wood. Reaching the door on the left, I pulled it open, finding a long table in the center of the room.

"What the fuck, Emma?" I heard Warden shout as he stood from the end of the table. Locking eyes with Hammer, I extended my hand holding the phone out to him.

"It's Detroit Memorial. Mrs. Flowers was in an accident with Liam. They can't find Kira." I faded off as Hammer launched himself over the table, snatching the phone from my hand.

The adrenaline dump hit me hard as several of his brothers followed Hammer out the door and into the lot. With labored breathing, the reality of what I'd done reared its ugly head as I rushed to get out of this forbidden place.

Crossing the concrete, I caught Hammer as he tossed the phone to Daxx before jumping into one of the trucks they used for part runs. Blue smoke billowed from the back tires in protest as Hammer fish-tailed out of the parking lot and through the gates.

"I've got to hand it to you. Emma. You've got balls." Farrah stood in the office doorway, a triumphant smile on her face. "Too bad your little stunt will cost you this job."

Stepping around her, I resumed my place behind the desk, concentrating on the spreadsheet on my computer.

"Need me to help you pack?"

Keeping my focus on the screen, I ignored the condescension in Farrah's attempted stab. "Have you ever heard the term play to the whistle?"

"No." She retorted, disbelief laced in the single word as if I'd made it up.

"It means you keep going until an official tells you to stop. Did I break a rule by going into that door?" Shifting my attention to Farrah, I pointed in the direction of the Clubhouse. "Yes," I slammed my hand on the desk. "Would I do it again?" My heart shattered for Hammer as he deals with what waits for him at the emergency room. "Absolutely."

Refusing to be the first to look away, I'm oddly thrilled when Daxx walked into the office.

"I believe this belongs to you." Spinning the phone in his hand, he shot me a sly smile as he placed it in the cradle on my desk. "Since you've taken over Syn's job for a while, can I ask a favor of you?"

Dumbfounded, I shifted my gaze between Daxx and Farrah, confusion riddling my mind. "Of course," I muttered, unsure of how this was possible.

"Come, let me show you something."

Hammer

CHAPTER
TWELVE
HAMMER

I FUCKING HATE HOSPITALS. You'd think for as many times as I'd sat in this waiting room, I'd be seasoned. But I'm not. It has nothing to do with the waiting, or the smell, but the look of fear in Liam's eyes, a fear I'm powerless to take away.

"She's still not answering, brother."

Raiden sat heavily in the seat beside me, tossing his cell to the table in front of us. He, along with several others, had been trying to get Kira on the phone for the last few hours. He'd beaten me to the emergency room, having heard Mrs. Flowers was involved.

"Thanks for trying."

Leaning back in my seat, I spear my fingers into the top of my head, tugging at the roots in an attempt to keep my shit together.

"What the fuck is taking them so long?"

They'd taken Liam for a CAT scan seemingly ages ago. It was precautionary, the doctor told me, due to the crash happening on his side of Mrs. Flowers' vehicle.

"I'll text Doc Ash if you'd like?" Erin's gentle voice preceded the touch of her hand to my thigh, her caress sending warmth to my chilly disposition. Liam had agreed to allow Doc Ash to go with him after she'd promised him a play date with her twins.

Shaking my head, I rose from the chair, crossing the room to the windows overlooking the city. The sun had been high in the sky when I'd first arrived, now the twinkling lights of downtown Detroit reflected back at me. Narrowing my gaze to the lights of one of the casinos, I allowed my mind to drift back to the moment Emma crashed through the door of the Clubhouse. We'd been discussing how Bolder, the president of Disciples of Destruction, was bragging about his club coming into a substantial amount of money. Daxx suggested perhaps they'd rekindled a relationship with the Cartel, however, Kannon suspected it had something to do with the still missing mafia princess.

"I found her."

Spinning on my heels, I found Warden standing inside the door, an angry look on his face.

"Where?" I demanded through clenched teeth, reminding myself no matter how bad I wanted to, I couldn't kill Kira.

"I put a call into our friend with the police department, who gave me Johnson's—"

"Where the fuck is my baby?" Kira's shrilling voice echoed down the hall a split second before she stomped into the room.

"Calm down, babe." Officer Johnson tried to reason as he trailed behind her. The poor bastard was in for a rude awakening if he thought Kira came with reasoning capability. "The nurse said his room was in..." Johnson trailed off as we locked gazes, recognition registering inside his blue orbs.

"Where is he?" Kira demanded as she surveyed the room. "That lying bitch," she seethed, her voice carrying down the hall.

"Hey," I called, snapping my fingers in her direction. "You can say whatever you want in the streets, but this is a hospital and you will be respectful. Now shut your whore mouth."

Johnson cleared his throat while stepping around Kira, closing the distance between us. "I'd appreciate it if you didn't call my girlfriend a whore."

Chuckling, I shook my head and took a couple steps of my own toward him. "Girlfriend? Kira doesn't know the definition. Trust me, she may be sucking your dick and calling you *meelyi*, but she sucks a lot of dick and calls every man love."

"Not anymore, Hammer." Johnson held up his hand. "I've taken the liberty of moving her belongings into my apartment and advised her to stop working at your strip club."

"Is that where you were, playing house with this guy instead of being available for our son?"

Kira's brows bent practically in half, her index finger pointed at me. "It was your time with him, not mine."

Her words didn't surprise me. Kira was quick to hand Liam off to anyone who would take him. "Doesn't give you an excuse to ignore your phone."

"I'm not using that cheap piece of shit you gave me." Kira admitted proudly, holding up a shiny new phone. "Ray gave me the one I asked you for."

Keeping my gaze locked with Johnson, the edge of my lips curled up in a grin. Kira was obsessed with shiny new things. When we first got together, I took great pride in giving her everything she wanted, until it wasn't enough. Her mind changed more often than the wind.

"And it never occurred to you to send me the number?"

"Don't put this on me, Hammer.We aren't together anymore, remember?"

Stepping closer to her, the closeness forced Kira to drop her hand. "Good luck with this one, Johnson. Not a responsible bone in her body." Dropping my focus to Kira's face.

"You're just jealous," Kira taunted, hooking her hands on her slender hips.

"Jealous?" I mimicked, huffing out a humorless laugh.

"Yes, jealous. Ray bought me the phone, and a new house, not far from the one I showed you."

Snapping my attention to Ray, "You bought a house in Sherwood Forest?"

"I've made an offer, yes." His answer was confident, yet cocky.

Drifting a quick glance in Raiden and Warden's direction, both nodded once before slipping out of the room. A few years ago, Kira came to me, begging to show me her absolute dream house. We'd driven out to one of the most expensive neighborhoods in Detroit, where she showed me the house. I'd made a few calls and was ready to buy it when Kannon did some digging and found out there was an issue with the owner owing back taxes. Kira was livid of course, spewing about how I didn't love her enough to pay the money. It was the last gift I'd ever considered buying her.

"Great neighborhood," I complimented, keeping to myself the question of how a man in his position could afford a house in such a prestigious neighborhood.

"Kira, sweetheart, I think I saw a coffee shop by the elevator." Reaching into his pocket, Ray pulled out a twenty and handed it to her. "Would you mind getting us something to drink?"

"For you," Kira reached up, placing a kiss to the edge of his lips. "Anything." The latter came out breathy, as if meant to torment me.

Ray waited until Kira stepped from the room before turning back to me. "Listen, I know the two of you have a long history, but I love her. The good, the bad, and especially the ugly. I want a family with her."

I could see where this conversation was headed. Johnson saw himself as a hero, riding in on his badge to save the damsel in distress from the evil biker. "She's free to do what she wants, but Liam is, and will always be, my son."

Ray held up his hands in surrender. "Of course, I would never…" He trailed off. "Now that you mentioned Liam, I would like to ask you to amend the custody agreement, giving Kira and I time to get the house together."

Ray's attempt at bargaining fell short with me. I knew what he was getting at. He wanted me to take our son so he could fuck his new girlfriend.

"Just for a few months, I swear," he added with a smile.

"The CT looks good, Hammer," Doc Ash announced as she crossed the threshold carrying a sleepy looking Liam. "This little button is good to go home."

Flashing a brief look in Johnson's direction. "One issue with your proposition, Ray," I called, crossing the room to take Liam from Doc

Ash's arms. "Mrs. Flowers won't be able to care for Liam for quite some time, considering her injuries. With Kira not working, she'll need to keep him during the day while I work."

Locking gazes with Doc Ash, I sent her a wink as I laid Liam on my chest. She'd agreed to be a professional witness if I needed her in my fight for sole custody.

"I'm sure—"

"Don't you dare assume since I'm not showing my tits for money, I'm not working." Kira ran into the room, shoving a cup of coffee into Ray's hand. "I have a house to furnish and...and..." She trailed off, her arms whipping around the room.

Reaching into my back pocket, I fished out my cell, keeping my eyes trained on Kira as I pressed speakerphone with my thumb.

"I thought you might have an issue with this." A triumphant smile splitting my face in half.

"*Hello, my sweet boy.*"

Kira's eyes grew wide as she recognized the voice. My mother was a special lady, one who, like Bullet's mom, didn't tolerate anyone's shit, especially Kira's.

"Hey, Mom, I need your help. How soon can you come to Michigan?"

Emma

CHAPTER
THIRTEEN
EMMA

MY FINGERS SHOOK as I placed the cereal boxes on the shelf. I'd spent the night waiting for Warden to call and tell me my services were no longer needed, but he never did.

"Play to the whistle," I reminded myself aloud, closing the cabinet door and moving to the rest of the groceries waiting on the counter to be put away.

Yesterday, Daxx showed me the empty cabinets in the small kitchen beside the sleeping quarters for the Club. Handing me a wad of cash, he'd asked me to go to the grocery store, something Syn had done weekly for him. Turns out, Daxx slept there when he wasn't spending the night with one of his regulars. He'd been detailed on what he wanted, and insisted I take notes on how to organize his food. I'd listened as he'd pointed out how the labels of the condiments and few remaining beverages were facing forward. Then, as if learning Daxx Inman was a card carrying OCD wasn't enough, he floored me when he'd shown me the recycling station he'd set up.

The discovery reminded me of another man I knew who had the same tendencies, although the similarity ended with the OCD.

"Emma?"

Spinning around, my hand flew to my chest, breath coming out in a sharp gasp.

"I didn't mean to startle you." The man with an intense set of green eyes stood with his hands raised in surrender. "I'm Kannon, by the way." Lowering his arms slowly, he extended his left one for me to shake.

"Oh," I smiled brightly, placing my hand in his. "You're Hailey's Kannon."

A smile commandeered his face, as a flush of happiness brightened his features. Kannon was without a doubt a handsome man with his dark hair and sharp jawline. I now understood why Hailey was so hesitant.

"I am now," Kannon squeezed my hand before releasing. "Thanks to you."

Tilting my head to the side, I leaned against the counter, crossing my arms over my chest. "How so?"

Mimicking my stance, Kannon crossed his ankles, dropping his gaze to the tile floor beneath our feet. "Yesterday, when Hailey came back to work, she asked if she could have a word with me in my office."

I watched as his eyes drifted up, his focus on the memory playing inside of his head.

"I'd assumed she found some information for me, however, once I closed the door..." His smile intensified, making him impossibly more attractive. Kannon shook his head before raising his gaze back to mine. "She kissed the shit out of me."

My hands flew to my mouth, my eyes wide with surprise.

"You have no idea how long I've dreamed of tasting that beautiful girl's lips."

His joy was contagious, nearly enough to rid me of the dread weighing me down. I'd be unemployed as soon as Warden came in. I'd heard Cisco telling the guys Hammer was picking his mother up from the airport this morning, no doubt using her to replace me.

"I'm not sure how I helped..."

Kannon reached out, grabbing one of the discarded bags and began to fold it. "The question you posed to her, about living in regret, gave her something to think about. Hailey stands on many principles, thankfully avoiding regret is one of them."

I thought back to the conversation Hailey and I shared, the look in her eyes moments before she bolted out of the door.

"Well, I'm glad I did some good yesterday." My voice cracked despite my best effort to contain it. I still had more than six months before my credentialing with the IRS would be complete and needed this job until then.

Tossing the bag to the side, Kannon laid his hand on my arm. "I was there, Emma. We weren't discussing anything of substance when you burst in."

"It's fine," I waved off. "I knew the consequences of my actions and did it anyway."

Nodding, Kannon dropped his hand to his side. "Do me a favor, Emma. Don't leave until you speak with Warden."

I could hear the tinkle of tiny laughter as I crossed the parking lot, followed by the gentle sound of a woman's voice. Taking a deep breath, I steeled myself before twisting the handle and entering the office

Crossing the threshold, the scene before me stopping me in my tracks, my heart leaving my chest and floating across the room. Hammer sat in my chair, a small child who was without a doubt the infamous Liam, a carbon copy of the much bigger man.

"Don't mess with Emma's files, son. She'll kick daddy's butt if you delete something."

Liam tipped his head back in laughter, his two front teeth highlighting his smile.

"You must be Emma?" A sweet voice sounded to my left, jerking my attention from the father and son moment, to the woman leaning against the file cabinet.

"Yes." Nodding, I held out my hand to her. For as much as Liam favored his father, this woman had many of his features.

"I'm Kathleen Sheppard, Hammer's momma."

I could see where Hammer got his intense eyes and perfect lips. Kathleen was a classic beauty who clearly took care of herself as it was hard to tell she was a grandmother.

"It's a pleasure to meet you. I'd be happy to show you the files, write down the passwords." The words came spilling out as I made to move toward the desk.

"Why on earth would I need to know this?"

Stopping in my tracks, looking from Hammer to Kathleen through confused eyes. "Because of…" I trailed off, feeling something tug at my skirt. Glancing down, I found Liam's bright blue eyes looking up at me, the stems of a bouquet of flowers grasped in his little hand, the blooms lying helplessly on the floor. "Here, let me help you." Bending down, I moved to right the flowers when Liam surprised me by letting the stem go, opening his arms wide and wrapping me in a hug.

"Tank you." He said into my ear, his toddler voice giving me a smile which warmed me to the core. Closing my eyes, I wrapped my arms around him, bathing in his sweet toddler scent.

"Ma, can you take Liam into the kitchen?"

Liam gripped me tighter, "No, Daddy, I wants Emma." He argued, burying his little face into my neck.

"Hey," I spoke softly as I pulled back. "Don't tell anyone, but I put some cookies in the cabinet above the refrigerator. Can you bring me one?"

Liam's eyes widened. Nodding with earnestness, he dropped his arms and turned toward Kathleen. "Come on, Nana."

Standing to my full height, I watched as the mini Hammer took Kathleen's hand, skipping as best he could out the door and into the parking lot.

"I need to talk with you about yesterday." Hammer's voice sounded behind me, making my eyes squeeze shut. This was it, the event I'd dreaded all night.

"I suspected as much," I admitted as I turned around. "Although I'd assumed it would be Warden here instead of you." Keeping my head up, I made my way around Hammer, "I don't regret what I did yesterday, even though it cost me this job."

"I'm not firing you."

Spinning on my heels, my mouth agape as his words registered in my mind. "But I…" I trailed off, pointing blindly to the building behind me.

"Tell me something, sweetheart." Hammer laid his hands on the desk, leaning his torso closer to me. "What color are the walls inside the club?"

"I..." Opening and closing my mouth several times, my mind drew a blank as to the answer to his question.

"How many men were in the room?"

Closing my eyes, I tried to picture the room. What color were the walls? Were there other men in the room?"

"I saw," I began. "No, I heard Warden." Correcting myself as I'd remembered hearing Warden shout my name.

Opening my eyes, I allowed my attention to drift to Hammer's handsome face. "I only saw you."

A heaviness filled the room, a sensual energy I've never felt before. The longing was reflected in Hammer's blue eyes, and I was lost in the gentle way each breath he exhaled caressed my face.

"I don't do regret either, darlin'." His admission was barely born before his warm lips connected with mine. Hammer took control of the kiss, cupping my face as he twisted my head to gain a better angle. The tiny voice inside my head was screaming for me to pull away, reminding me how bad an idea this was. However, it's the louder voice, the one reminding me I am a woman with pent up carnal desires. With my inner battle over, I moved my hands to his chest, exploring the firm lines of his muscular torso, soaking in the moans which vibrated from within him.

"No one is more grateful than me for what you did." He whispered against my lips, his teeth nipping at my lower lip.

"So I'm not fired?" The lameness of my question caused my body to flinch, and Hammer to pull away.

"No, babe," he smacked his lips against mine a second time before standing and crossing the room. "Definitely not fired." He added with a wink before stepping from the room.

Touching my fingertip to my lips, the sensation of his kiss still lingering as I watched Hammer walk across the parking lot. Falling heavily in my seat, I continued to stare as Liam and Kathleen came out of the Clubhouse door. Liam extended a hand holding what looked like a cookie. Hammer bent over, scooped up a smiling Liam and tossed him over his shoulders. Laughter erupted from my throat as I heard a joyous squeal from Liam as Hammer began to tickle him.

"Melts your ovaries, doesn't it?"

Snapping my gaze to the left, I found Kira standing against the wall, an extra-long manicured fingernail trapped between her front teeth.

"Although I remember you swore you had no intention of getting involved with Hammer."

"Funny," I huffed, spinning my chair toward the computer. "I remember you telling me the two of you were married."

Kira dropped her hand to her side, a sinister smile crossing her lips. "Touché," she nodded her head. "Although I must admit watching the two of you kiss was fucking hot."

Balancing her arms on the desk, her ample chest on full display in front of me. "I'd love to see the look on your face when he eats your pussy."

Standing to my full height, I locked gazes with Kira. In the short time I'd known her, I'd come to realize she was much like Macy, a bully.

"Is there something I can help you with? Besides adding to your spank bank, that is."

"From you, I doubt it, honey." Kira huffed, shifting her gaze to the now empty parking lot. Just like Macy, the moment Kira was shown a valid challenge, she shifted gears. "I stopped by to say hello to Kathleen."

Somehow I doubted that. According to the conversations I'd heard, no one, not even Hammer, liked Kira. "Are you even capable of telling the truth?"

"What?" Kira looked me up and down, her upper lips raised in disgust. "Kathleen loves me."

Shaking my head, I tucked my skirt under me as I dropped into my chair. "Keep telling yourself that, Kira. You're the only one who will believe it."

"You don't fucking know me," Kira slammed her hand on the desk.

"One kiss from Hammer and you think you know everything." Rounding the desk, Kira bent her upper body, bringing her nose within millimeters of mine. "Hammer kisses a lot of bitches, fucks even more. Don't fool yourself, he won't lie awake tonight and think about you. He'll be too busy with the next girl he bumps into."

Keeping my tone even, "You know, Kira. I can't decide if your shitty attitude is a result of jealousy or a bad case of constipation. By that wrinkle in the center of your forehead, I'm guessing the latter." Turning toward my computer, "Now, if you'll excuse me."

"He's like a merry go round," Kira barked through clenched teeth, her hand slamming into my shoulder stopping me in my tracks. "Every bitch on the block has had a turn riding him."

Reaching over, I removed her hand from my shoulder. "If that were true, you wouldn't be here fighting so hard for him. Face it, Kira. You don't want him, but you don't want anyone else to have him either. Don't you think it's time to move on?"

"You'd like that, wouldn't you? Have me out of the picture so you can claim..." She trailed off, realization flashing in her eyes as if she'd almost said too much.

"Claim what?" I demanded.

Kira adjusted her stance, a stoic look taking over her face. "Stay the fuck away from my family." Emphasizing each word through clenched teeth. "Or you will wish you were never born."

Hammer

CHAPTER FOURTEEN

HAMMER

"SON, you know I would rather cut off my tongue than to interfere in your life."

"But?" I deadpanned, looking at my sleeping child in the rearview mirror.

"I saw the kiss, Hammer."

"I've kissed a lot of girls, Ma. What's your point?" I hadn't planned on kissing Emma like I did. She wasn't like Kira or Roxie. She was smart and kind, and, sadly, would move on to better things once Syn had her baby. Despite all that, I wanted her. Not just to suck my dick like the others, but something on a level I never thought I'd reach.

"My point is, you're about to go into the legal battle of your life. Do you think hitching your horse to a woman you barely know is a good idea?" She whispered, chancing a glance over her shoulder at Liam.

"Do you not like Emma?" My question was redundant as I'd seen the look on her face as she approached Emma, and heard the tenderness in her voice as she introduced herself.

"She practically saved my grandbaby, how can I not like her?" She mumbled as she turned her head to stare out the window.

"Listen, Ma, I need you to trust me on this one. There are things about Emma you don't know and we, as a Club, have chosen not to share."

My mother's gaze snapped to mine, her eyes surveying my face. "She reminds me of myself when I met your father. Skirt to my ankles and full of innocence." A smile split her face in two as she turned her attention to the front of the car. "Must be a Sheppard trait to pursue the woman least like them."

I'd heard the story from my grandmother of how my mother was the quintessential girl next door when she'd met my father.

"I don't know about any family traits, but I do recall you telling me the heart doesn't ask permission when it decides to fall in love."

Ma shook her head before turning back to me. "Promise me something, Jonathan."

My heart rate increased when my given name dropped from her lips. She'd adapted my road name easily from the moment I'd earned it.

"Give Emma the same respect you give your brothers."

"What the hell, Kannon? You gonna play or what?"

Tossing my cards to the side, I turned my attention to the opposite side of the table to find Kannon wiping his hands over his face.

"Sorry," he mumbled, voice thick with exhaustion. Tossing two cards into the center of the table. "Haven't had much sleep in the last few days." He added as Daxx slid two cards in his direction. The speck of a smile not getting passed me.

"Something keeping you up?" Warden called from the corner of the room, his brows bent in concern. "Need a visit from one of the girls?"

Leaning back in my chair, I watched as Kannon's smile grew, a happiness coating his face I'd never seen.

"Nah, Warden," he shook his head, tossing a handful of poker chips to the pile. "My lack of sleep is for the best fucking reason."

Snapping my focus to Daxx, I found the same confusion swimming in his eyes. "Something we need to know, man?"

Kannon stared at the grains of the table for several tense filled seconds before raising his gaze to mine. "In all the years I've been with this Club, I've had at least a dozen women tell me they wanted to fuck my brains out. Several have come close, making me see stars while I shot a load down their throats."

Shaking his head, Kannon turned his attention to Daxx sitting beside him. "Not one of them, not a single fucking chic in the Club, has ever made me lose myself in them."

Reaching for my beer, my interest piqued as to what the fuck had changed in my Club brother.

"Two days ago, I was standing in my office preparing for a court appearance I had to make, when my door slammed open and Hailey stood there looking beautiful like she always does. Next thing I knew, she'd launched herself at me, laying a kiss on my lips I won't ever forget."

My mind rushed back to the kiss I'd laid on Emma and how I'd spent the night thinking of all the ways I wanted to show her how I felt. I'd been unable to talk with her since as Warden and I had been preparing for our meeting with Ace. He'd canceled at the last minute the other night, gifting us with more time to get our shit together.

"She apologized for being stupid and not realizing how much I meant to her. She's spent the last forty-eight hours making up for all the time we've lost." Kannon finished, running his thumb along his bottom lip, the memories shining brightly on his face.

"Wait a fucking minute," I shouted from my seat. "Our Hailey?" I clarified, knowing the sweet girl we'd rescued last year had refused anything other than a professional relationship with Kannon.

"She's *my* Hailey, actually." Emphasizing the possession. "Thanks to Emma."

"Fucking Emma," Daxx swore under his breath, gaining my attention.

"What do you mean, 'fucking Emma'?" Not giving two shits how lethal my words sounded.

Daxx's gaze snapped to mine, his eyes perusing my face, brows bent in curiosity. "Apparently, there is a baby shower planned for Syn tomorrow night."

"Does my sister know this?"

Layla took a great deal of pride in planning most of the parties for the Club. I knew for fact she was working overtime planning a surprise baby shower for Syn in a few months.

Daxx tilted his head back, letting out an exasperated breath. "I told Syn this was a fucking bad idea." He swore, leveling his face in my direction. "I doubt it, since Tiffany called while I was driving Syn to her ultrasound appointment. She told her to have the tech put the results in an envelope so they could announce it at the party they were throwing for her. Syn told Tiffany specifically not to invite Emma."

Slamming my eyes shut, I struggled to maintain my temper. When would this bitch learn to keep her mouth shut?

"When and where is this fucking party?" Warden's deep voice forced my eyes open.

"Tomorrow night, in the Bitch Room."

Shifting my attention to Warden, my anger rose once again. Years ago, one of the hang-arounds cleaned out one of the storage rooms which the Club had forgotten about. She turned it into a space where the girls could keep clothes and shit they needed. They labeled it the Bitch Room and it stuck.

"Motherfucker," he swore, standing to his feet and tossing the bottle of beer in his hand into the trash. Spearing his fingers into the top of his head, Warden stood staring at the empty wall beside him. "Did you tell them it was okay to have a party, Daxx?"

"Have we ever questioned what the fuck they did back there?"

Pinching the bridge of his nose, Warden pulled out his phone and touched the screen.

"*What do you want?*" Farrah's voice echoed from the speaker.

"Syn's party tomorrow night. What do you know about it?"

"*Awe, so the shit has hit the fan, has it?*" Farrah laughed, the sound of music in the background.

"Not what I asked, Farrah."

"*I have nothing to do with it, Warden. I got a group text this morning from Tiffany. I declined, so did Erin and Jillian. Layla's pissed, but she's going.*"

"Why aren't you going?"

"*Because I have plans,*" Farrah deadpanned.

"Cancel them. I need you at this party."

"*I—*"

"It's not a request, Farrah. Ace McKenzie is in town and I need you to hurry this baby shit along before he arrives."

I expected Farrah to give a colorful retort. Warden had confided in me despite her apology to Erin, he couldn't bring himself to rekindle his marriage. While the word divorce had yet to leave his lips, I had zero doubt it was running through his mind.

"*I'll do my best, but you know how those bitches can be. Especially if Kira decides to tell everyone about Hammer kissing Emma.*"

Emma

CHAPTER
FIFTEEN
EMMA

GRIPPING the handle of the bag, I pulled it from the trunk of my car and closed the hatch. Steadying my nerves, I reminded myself of the promise I'd made Jillian and Erin before learning I was purposely left off the guest list of Syn's party.

"Five minutes, Emma. Put the gift on the table and hightail it out of here," I whispered, an encouragement to myself I could do this. As I moved to step around the back of the car, I caught the sound of laughter. Searching the parking lot, my gaze landed on Hammer as he carried a woman over his shoulder across the concrete toward the building.

"Hammer stop." The woman playfully warned, swatting at his ass as he opened the door and stepped over the threshold.

Dipping my head to the ground, I took a deep breath, before squaring my shoulders and walking with purpose toward the back of the warehouse.

I'd managed to come up with a million excuses for why Hammer had avoided me the past few days. Seems Kira was right when she'd said he kissed a lot of girls and wouldn't give me a second thought.

It was one kiss, Emma, not a property patch. I shivered as I thought the words, the implication of their meaning never bothering me more than this moment.

Nearing the door, I moved to grip the handle when a hand slammed on the metal in front of me.

"Where the fuck do you think you're going?" Shifting my gaze from the acrylic fingernails to the overly-made up face of the blonde beside me. I recognized Syn from the multitude of photos I'd found in the office.

Recognition flashed on Syn's face, her eyes narrowing as she crossed her arms over her ample chest. "So, you're the gash who is trying to steal my job."

Gash? I hadn't been called that colorful term of endearment in a while.

"Listen, Syn, I'm here to deliver these gifts." Raising the bag in my hand. "I know you don't want me here. As far as your job, I'm filling in until you have the baby and not a second longer."

Tension filled the space between us as Syn surveyed me from top to bottom. She was a beautiful girl, with long blonde hair and ample assets. Like Macy, she was sexy without trying.

"I heard you turned on the computers," Syn nodded toward my office behind me. "Started using checks to pay the bills."

Setting the bag at her feet, "It's called working harder not smarter. You'll thank me if the IRS ever audits the company."

"Is that what they teach you in college?" Syn's tone was condescending, an attempt to make me feel bad about being educated. She wasn't the first, and I doubted she'd be the last.

"Among other things," I shrugged, giving her nothing to fuel her fire.

"Well," Syn took a step closer. "I bet they didn't teach you it's a bad idea to hitch yourself to a man like Hammer."

"I—" I began but Syn interrupted.

"Kira and Hammer have a history that runs deep, one only they can fully understand. They fight and they fuck, hell sometimes they fight so they can fuck. They have a habit of letting the other have a little side action, something to stir up the jealousy to make things steamy when they get back together."

A devilish smile flashed across Syn's lips, "And trust me, Emma, they *always* come back together."

Taking a breath ready to argue, Syn dropped her arms, her hand caressing her rounded belly.

"Wanna know why Hailey chose not to be with Kannon?" She continued. "Because she knows she doesn't fit into our world. Just like you don't," her voice sounded triumphant. However, as if on cue, Kannon pulled his bike into the parking lot, the engine barely off before he pulled Hailey in for a heated kiss

"You were saying?" Pointing at the couple in question, not bothering to hide the grin on my face. Turning back to the couple, I find Hailey waving in my direction, Kannon wrapped around her back with his lips attached to her neck as they walked toward us

Swallowing back a bite of jealousy, I refused to give Syn anything to take back to Kira. What had happened between Hammer and I may have been a game to them, but I refused to be a player anymore.

"What the fuck?"

Turning my attention back to Syn, I was about to explain how Hailey and Kannon were now a couple when the door to the warehouse flew open, a shocked Layla standing in the threshold.

"There you are, Syn. We were getting worried about you."

Letting out a breath I didn't realize I was holding, I moved to step back when Layla's gaze caught mine. "Your friends are waiting for you." She encouraged Syn as she reached out and grabbed my arm preventing me from going anywhere. Layla waited until Syn disappeared down the hall before rounding on me.

"Oh my God, you guys!" Layla's huge eyes bore into mine. "You have no idea how embarrassing this party is."

"What do you mean?" Hailey spoke from beside me, her ever-present concern lacing in her words

"There's no food, only copious amounts of beer. Don't get me started on the hideous decorations." She emphasized by rolling her beautiful eyes.

"Well, that's what they get for not putting you in charge." When Layla came by this morning in a huff looking for Hammer, she'd broken the news of the gender reveal. Opening my arms wide, I moved to hug Hailey. "Have fun," I feigned enthusiasm.

"Wait," Layla exclaimed. "You're leaving?"

"I wasn't invited, remember?"

"Fuck that, I'm inviting you. I will need both of your help to pull this thing off."

"Seriously, Layla? This party may not be up to your standards, but it was thrown by her friends with her in mind." I reminded her, bending down for the gift bag Syn left behind.

"Now, if you don't mind, I'm going—"

"This isn't about tacky decorations," Layla interrupted. "Okay, maybe a little. But it's more about the Club's reputation, specifically my brother and Warden."

I wanted to remind her Hammer's reputation was sullied before this party was even thought of, but I held my tongue.

"Based on the story Kira is spewing in there about my brother kissing your ass off, I mistakenly assumed you'd be willing to help."

"You could always ask the girl he carted in over his shoulder. I'm sure he has her sprawled out on his bed at the back of the Club." The clipped words were out of my mouth before I could retract them.

"You mean Dr. Anderson?" Layla jammed her thumb over her shoulder. "Pretty blonde with ridiculously high heels?"

I hadn't allowed myself to study the pair, too angry at the time I'd wasted in worrying why he hadn't contacted me.

"I guess," I shrugged.

"Dr. Anderson is the team doctor for the Detroit Northman. Her stepfather is a Meidani," Layla allowed the infamous last name to hang in the air. Ignoring the syndicate portion of her confession, I focused on the physician part of the equation.

"Is someone hurt?"

Layla smiled, shifting her gaze to Hailey's before returning it to mine. "When Erin got the text about this party, she suggested Doc Ash come and do the DNA tests for the paternity of Syn's baby since all parties would be in the same room. Doc Ash wasn't available, but she called in a favor from her friend, Doc Anderson, to come help."

Staring at Layla through confused eyes, "And this Dr. Anderson has trouble walking?"

Adjusting her stance, Layla reached out laying her hand on my shoulder. "Ever worn heels to work, Emma?"

Shaking my head adamantly, "I don't own any heels."

"Well, I do. Nothing compared to the kind Dr. Anderson wears, and I can tell you the parking lot is full of small cracks. Hammer is a natural-born protector and given who her family is." Layla trailed off, but the explanation didn't need to be said.

"So, are you going to help me or not?"

Feeling foolish, I shot Layla a smile, "Of course. What do you need me to do?"

Clapping her hands together, "Thank fuck. I have an order on its way from a local restaurant and I need your help getting everything set up."

Gripping my wrist in her hands, "Come on, Emma. We have an important guest to impress and not a lot of time to do it."

Hammer

CHAPTER
SIXTEEN
HAMMER

"ALRIGHT, MOTHERFUCKERS," Warden clapped his hands together as he entered the room. "Ace just texted me, he's on his way. I need everyone, with the exception of Raiden, to head over to the Club house and let Doc Anderson get a sample of your DNA before he gets here."

Shifting my attention from the screen of my phone to my brother's less than enthused face. "Fuck," I muttered under my breath before letting my head fall to my chest.

"No, you fucking don't." Stoney's gravely voice barked from behind the bar. I snapped my attention toward him, just as he tossed a towel to the top of the bar.

"Sorry, old man," Warden looked in Stoney's direction, and I could tell he was holding back a smile. "This doesn't concern you."

"The fuck it doesn't," Stoney rounded the bar, taking deliberate steps to come face to face with Warden. "Syn's baby is mine."

Silence filled the room as every eye landed on the man most of us considered a father.

"How the...?" I trailed off, pocketing my phone and closing the distance between us.

"It was the night of Raiden's party," Stoney began. My gaze flashed to Daxx and Bullet who slowly approached. "I found her crying in her car after Daxx left with Sasha and a couple of other girls. I took her home with the intention of cooking her a decent meal and encouraging her to find someone who returned her feelings."

It was no secret Syn wanted to be property patched by any brother who was willing. Which is the sole reason everyone, with the exception of Raiden, needed a test.

"One thing led to another."

"Hold on, Dad," Daxx held up his hand, his eyes closed and face contorted in a scowl. "Is this even possible? I mean you're…"

"Old?" Stoney finished for him.

"Well, yes." Daxx speared his fingers into the top of his head, tugging at the roots of his hair.

"Listen, son, just because there is snow on the roof doesn't mean there isn't a fire inside."

Spinning on his heels, Daxx raised his hands in the air. "Fuck me!" He shouted into the room. "Syn's kid is my…"

"Little brother or sister," Stoney finished again. "Which I'd really like to find out if you fuckers don't mind." He added, pointing toward the wall which separated us from the Bitch Room.

I watched as Daxx turned around, a defeated look on his face. Taking two deliberate steps, Daxx extended his hand to his father. "Congratulations, Pops."

Everyone remained silent as Stoney pulled Daxx in for a back-slapping hug.

"Anyone home?" A familiar voice called from the doorway.

"Ace," Warden called, extending his hand as he swiftly cleared the distance. "You're early."

Several men stood behind Ace, a hand selected group to offer him protection. I was familiar with the first two, but the remaining three were a mystery to me.

"Yes, my business concluded early. I assumed you wouldn't mind if I came on over."

"It's fine, Ace. You're always welcome." Warden motioned to the table in the center of the room, "Please, have a seat."

Falling in step behind Warden, we waited for Ace to choose a seat before we taking ours.

"I suppose you're all curious as to why I'm here?" Ace spoke to the room, several heads nodding in return. "Well," he smiled, lacing his fingers together on the table. "I'm doing a tour of several of the chapters to see how you are doing."

Sharing a look with Warden, we'd both been sworn to secrecy as to his retirement. If word got out before a successor was chosen, it could get messy.

"And how are they?" Warden mimicked Ace's position.

"Some are better than others." Ace spoke cryptically. "Tell me, Warden, did Linx repay the loan you extended?"

Keeping my reaction in check, as I wasn't aware Ace knew of the arrangement we had with Linx.

"Most of it," Warden nodded his head as he spoke each word.

"Most, but not all?" Ace's question left me with an uneasy feeling, something I would discuss with Warden once Ace left.

"No," Warden adjusted in his chair. "But it's all good."

"So you forgave the balance?"

"It wasn't much, besides Linx and I go way back." Linx and Warden grew up together. Hell, I'm surprised Linx wasn't VP instead of me.

"So you trust him?"

"What's this about?"

Several tense seconds ticked away as the two presidents locked gazes. Warden was never one to back down from anything, yet Ace didn't get his position by being a doormat.

"I noticed there was a party going on when I came in. What are we celebrating?"

It didn't escape me when Ace failed to answer Warden's question, another point I'd bring up later.

"A baby shower or some shit," Warden waved off. "One of the hang-arounds is expecting and the girls wanted to throw her a party."

I watched as Ace moved to rebut when the door to the room opened and a nervous looking Keys stepped into the room.

"What's wrong, Keys?" Warden was already standing as the question left his mouth. I followed suit as the hairs on the back of my neck stood up.

"I need y'all to come to the office. We have a situation on our hands."

"Can't you handle it, Keys?" Ace's voice sounded incredulous, as the majority of us were already headed toward the door.

"Not when these girls are involved."

Stepping around Keys, I took off in a run, heading for the Bitch Room. My fear was Syn and her friends had done something to Emma. I'd been watching her on the security cameras as she'd attempted to drop off a gift. Despite feeling like a voyeur, I'd continued to watch as she helped my sister unload food for Ace's party.

Farrah stood outside the room, her arms crossed and a disgusted look on her face. "I tried to tell them, Warden."

I heard her say as I rounded the corner and stepped into the room. I stopped short as I took in the sight before me. Syn stood beside a large box, decorated with pink and blue wrapping paper, as blue balloons floated to the ceiling.

"It's a boy!" Syn exclaimed, her voice rising high enough to make dog's howl. Stoney stood not far from her, a contented smile on his face.

"What the—" I began, rounding on Keys when I noticed Ace looking at the hall behind us.

"Ace?" I heard Emma's voice question. "What are you doing here?"

Crossing the short distance to the hall, I found Emma holding a case of alcohol, her brows furrowed in confusion.

"What am I doing here?" Ace returned, moving toward her with his arms raised. "What are you doing here? Last I heard you were living with that Clark guy." Ace took the case from her, handing it to one of his men, before pulling her into a hug.

"You know her?" Warden spoke the question on my lips as my shock had rendered me silent.

"This is my daughter."

Emma

CHAPTER
SEVENTEEN
EMMA

MY HEARTBEAT QUICKENED as I allowed Ace to envelope me in a hug. I'd never intended for anyone to find out my attachment to an outlaw biker. It had taken the better part of five years for Ace to win me over after he'd patched my mother and then married her. I'd refused to take his name or allow him to pay for college, as deep down, I still held him responsible for so many things.

"Emma, you should have told us." Warden spoke softly from behind my step father.

"Not her style, Warden. Emma makes it a point to pave her own way." He added, placing a kiss to my forehead before pulling away. "Mind telling me why you're in one of my chapter clubs? I seem to recall—"

The shrill of my cellphone interrupted his question. Taking the distraction as a life-line, I pulled the phone from my pocket, not caring if it was a scammer on the other end.

"Hello?" I spoke into the phone, holding up my index finger toward the men in front of me.

"*This is a collect call from,*" The robotic voice began sending my heart into my throat. "*Macy,*" I heard my sister's voice. "*An inmate in the*

Oakland County Jail. Press one to accept or..." I didn't wait for a second option as I lowered my phone and pressed the number.

"It's Macy," I whispered, raising the phone back to my ear as I waited for it to connect.

"Fuck," I heard Ace swear and the distinct sound of Hammer asking who Macy was.

Turning my back to them, I shoved my finger into my free ear to help me hear the call.

"Emma?" My sister screamed into the phone.

"Yes, Macy, I'm here. What's going on?"

"I'm in jail. Please, you have to come get Jackson. They're threatening to send him to foster care if you're not here within the hour."

"Wait, why are you in Detroit?"

"I'll tell you when you get here, if they let me see you."

"Tell me now," I demanded, but was met with silence.

Pulling the phone away from my ear, I confirmed Macy had indeed hung up.

"What does she want, Emma? Money?"

"She needs me to come get Jackson." Pocketing my phone, I raised my gaze to Ace, "Apparently, she is in jail." Holding his gaze for a moment. "In Detroit."

"This is all my fault." Ace pinched the bridge of his nose before letting out a strangled breath. "I paid a visit to Boulder earlier this week."

"You didn't?" I exclaimed, wanting nothing more than to hit Ace as hard as I could.

"I'm so sorry to interrupt," Hailey's sweet voice called from behind Ace, tamping down my rising anger. "But it sounds like you need a lawyer."

"No—"

"Yes," I pointed at Ace, my eyes wide in defiance. "We do." Keeping my eyes trained on him, I reached out for Hailey. "You're familiar with Oakland County jail, correct?"

"I am," Hailey assured, her cautious eyes searching mine. "However,

I need to stop by my office and grab paperwork for temporary custody of...?" She rolled her hand, silently asking for his name again.

"Jackson," shifting my gaze from Hailey's face to Hammer's. "My nephew."

"I'll go with you," Hammer offered as he stepped forward.

"No," Ace shook his head. "This is my fuck up, I'll go."

"Um," Warden held his phone up to Hammer. "I second Hammer going. According to this, Boulder was stabbed earlier tonight. He's at Presbyterian hospital in the ER. If what I'm thinking happened, Emma and Hailey will need our protection."

"So is this Clark guy your boyfriend?"

"Really?" I laughed, keeping my attention on the taillights of the car in front of us. "That's your first question, Hammer? Not, why didn't I tell you about Ace?"

"I *know* who Ace is," Hammer emphasized, reaching over and taking my hand.

"Not very well apparently, you didn't know he had a family." I retorted, feeling instantly guilty for being rude.

"Answer my question, please."

Lacing my fingers with his, I tried to relax into the leather seat. "Clark Bruce was the teacher's assistant in my tax law class. He came from money, his family owns one of the largest accounting firms in the country. I was attracted to the nerdy vibe he had, so when he asked me out, I jumped on it."

Turning my head toward Hammer, I took in the massive man beside me. He was such a contradiction to my past relationships, all muscle and steel instead of boring and calculated.

"I learned fairly quickly Clark suffered from extreme OCD tendencies, so much more than Daxx. He'd tugged on my heartstrings when he shared the amount of therapy and medication it took to help him function." Letting out a huff I used my free hand to comb through my ponytail. I'd kept to myself how Clark used his illness as an excuse to keep us from becoming intimate.

"We'd been dating for about a month when Clark sat me down and showed me a timeline of his expectations for the progression of our relationship. I found it cute at the time, and wasn't surprised when he followed the timeline to the letter. Our first kiss, meeting the parents."

Hammer remained silent, softly rubbing his thumb along the top of my knuckles.

"When the time for an engagement grew closer, I anticipated he would do it at his family's Christmas Eve party. I'd bought a new dress and practiced how I would react when he dropped to one knee. However, the night in question grew later and Clark still hadn't asked, his oldest sister asked me to help her put the children to sleep. I was headed back to the living room when I heard Clark and his brother talking. He'd asked Clark when he planned to ask me to marry him, and Clark said I was the wife their parents wanted, not him."

I'd felt as if I'd been kicked in the stomach as I stood in the dark kitchen, having given up a large part of myself to fit into his precious timeline.

"His brother asked what his plan for me was. Clark said he was going to make the breakup my fault, that way he remained the perfect son in his parents eyes. I went back to the family room and began plotting the ultimate breakup."

I shivered as I thought of how my skin crawled when I wished Clark a Merry Christmas, placing a kiss to his cheek a few hours later.

"Which was?" Hammer kissed the back of my hand, his sweet smell bringing me back to the moment.

"His father's birthday was the following week. I'd hired an actress to come to the party and confront Clark. She shared details about him, nothing too personal, but enough to convince the family he was unfaithful to me. I broke up with him, gave the actress a ride home and haven't spoken with Clark until a few days ago."

"What did he want?"

"His last semester of college, he'd interned with the IRS, which ironically is the reason I applied to work with them. Anyway, he spoke with

an old colleague who mentioned he'd come across my credential applica-
tion. Then he asked if I was free to have a drink with him."

When Hammer stopped rubbing my hand, I chanced a glance in his
direction. He sat staring out the driver's side window, a deep valley
between his brows.

"Did you agree to meet him?" His voice was low and unsure, the
complete opposite of the Hammer I knew.

"I said I was swamped at work, and I would get back to him once
things cleared up a bit."

Hammer moved his focus to the car in front of us. Mumbling something under his breath I couldn't understand as he cut through traffic.

"I didn't ask you about Ace," Hammer began, his voice tense,
knuckles turning white. "Because I already knew you had an affiliation
with him."

"Hailey." Her name dropped from my lips as Hammer pulled into
the parking lot of the jail. I couldn't fault her, she was after all, protecting
the men who saved her.

"Roxie actually," he admitted, shutting off the car and turning toward
me. "What I'm about to tell you stays in this car, understand me?"

Nodding my head, I swallowed hard and squared my shoulders. I'm
no stranger to secrets the Club keeps, and the ramifications of betraying
your word. "I understand."

"Roxie came to me the other night, she is," Hammer trailed off, his
eyes dropping to our tangled hands.

A club whore.

A rocket scientist.

A closet organizer.

I thought to myself as I waited for Hammer to finish his sentence.

"An informant for the Club."

"Roxie?" I echoed back, disbelief coating my words.

Hammer nodded, a slip of a smile coating his lips. "She's been
feeding us information about a rival Club."

"Roxie?" I repeated, mentally picturing the woman who'd sat across
from me at lunch. While I agreed she looked the part of a hang-around,
her petite stature caused me concern.

"She told me she saw a picture of you and whom I assuming is your sister tucked away in the drawer of someone we are watching."

He didn't need to say the name of the man, I already knew. Hollister Banks aka Boulder.

"Come on, Sweetheart. Let's go get your nephew."

My heart raced as Hammer led me down a myriad of hallways and finally to a desk at the end of a corridor. He'd spoken with nearly every uniformed individual we'd passed, proof positive he'd been here many times.

"How can I help you?" The portly man behind the desk mumbled around a bite of a donut. Powdered sugar covered his fingers and a dollop of a red substance rested on his name badge, obscuring his name.

"We're here to see," Hammer trailed off, shifting his gaze to me.

"Macy," I whispered in disbelief, confused as to why he didn't seem to know the man behind the desk. "Macy Shaw." I spoke a little louder as the man sat the donut down, licking the sugar off his digits.

"And you are?"

"They're with me," Hailey's voice sounded behind me a second before she handed the man a laminated card. "You should have received a call from your supervisor of our impending arrival."

Gone was the timid woman who stood in my office not long ago, in her place was a professionally dressed, confident woman, ready to take on the world. With her dark hair pulled back in a severe bun, wearing a green silk shirt that made her eyes stand out against her porcelain face.

"I um..." The man uttered, clearly as shocked as I was at the confidence rolling off Hailey.

"You what, Officer Reynolds? Need a napkin and a letter of failure to due process in your file?" Hailey raised a brow over her left eye in challenge.

"Damn, Sis, no wonder Kannon is all twisted up about you." Hammer wagged his eyebrows, leaning against the counter, his appreciative gaze sparking a hint of jealousy inside me.

"Well?" Hailey demanded, clearly ignoring Hammer and his flirting. "My client is waiting."

Macy looked much thinner than the last time I'd seen her. Her blonde hair, which once matched mine, was now a mix of brassy yellow and faded pink and purple. Her cheeks were hollow and the dark circles under her eyes made her look ill. Her lips were chapped and her fingernails were jagged and bitten into the quick.

"Hey, Emma, thanks for coming."

"You're my sister," I chastised. "Of course I came." Sliding into the seat across from her, I took her hands in mine. "Now, tell me why you're in Detroit."

Macy nodded her head toward me. "Who are they?"

Glancing over my shoulder at Hammer. "This is my," hesitating, I wasn't certain what to call him. Boss? Friend? Certainly one kiss didn't make him anything more.

"Jonathan Sheppard," Hammer stepped forward. "Most folks call me Hammer. I'm your sister's boyfriend."

"Boyfriend?" Macy's gaze snapped to mine. "Since when did you start walking on the wild side?"

Choosing not to answer, since in reality I didn't have one. "This is my friend, and your attorney, Hailey Little."

"I can't pay you," Macy blurted out. For the first time I saw the missing teeth in the front of her mouth, and the blood staining the inside of her lips.

"I'm not asking you to. Emma is my dearest friend and I owe her an enormous favor." Hailey circled the table, placing her slender hip on the edge. "Now, tell me why we're here."

Macy dropped her head, taking several measure breaths. "I was hanging out with this guy I've been seeing. Nothing serious, just a getting high together kind of thing." She shrugged as if this were a normal thing, which in her world, it was.

"He'd scored some blow that was supposed to be amazing shit, but when we sat down to do it, he told me I had to suck his dick if I wanted any. I got pissed off, grabbed Jackson and took his car keys. Next thing I know, I'm on the outskirts of Detroit. I had a basic idea of where Boulder lived, so I made my way there."

Macy had been in love with Hollister since the minute she'd laid eyes on him. Ace tried to discourage the relationship, but Macy was determined and Hollister was horny.

"He was with another girl, but whatever." Macy rolled her eyes, a knowing smile touching her lips. "Wouldn't be the first time we'd had other people join us. Anyway, instead of inviting me in, he told me to take my bastard baby and leave. Said he'd signed his rights away and I was someone else's problem. I called him an asshole and stabbed him with my car keys three times in his dick."

"Did you say anything to the arresting officer or the detective?" Hailey fired off before I could say anything.

"Fuck no, but they're threatening to send Jackson to social services." Shifting her gaze to mine, those pleading eyes boring into mine. "You have to take him, Emma. I can't have him with strangers."

A part of me wanted to remind her of all the times she'd left him with strangers. Of how he'd memorized my phone number and would steal a phone to call me.

"Listen to me, Macy, don't say anything to anyone. I'll make sure Jackson goes to stay with your sister. You won't see the judge until tomorrow, but I'll be there to get your bond set and out of this place."

Macy dropped my hands, leaning back in the plastic chair. "I don't have money for bail."

"Ace has volunteered to handle any expenses," Hailey assured. "You should know, Ace is the one who paid Boulder to sign away his rights. He said to tell you it was Club business."

Hammer

CHAPTER
EIGHTEEN

HAMMER

RAIN HAD BEGUN to fall as I stepped into the back lot of the jail. Meeting Emma's sister had been a complete mindfuck. Where Emma was reserved and modest, Macy was the poster child for everything wild and chaotic.

Reaching into my pocket, I retrieved my phone, ready to dial my mother and recruit her help when it began to ring. Noticing the name across the screen, I dropped my head back as I raised the phone to my ear.

"It's late, Kira. What do you want?"

"Awe, does Mary Poppins make you go to bed early now?" She laughed. Kira hated rules, having never met a boundary she hadn't crossed.

"Tell me what the fuck you want, or I'm hanging up." I didn't have time for her antics. I needed to get things ready for Jackson.

"Fine. I need a favor."

"Not interested. Hanging up now."

"Wait!" She screamed, forcing me to pull the phone away from my ear. *"Ray's family is coming to town and they want to meet Liam. I know you said you'd keep him for the next three months, but I need to push it back a few weeks."*

It was a good thing I'd known Kira for so long as I barely caught half of what she'd spewed out.

"Awe, are we trying to be June Cleaver?" I teased back.

"Who?"

I'd forgotten Kira didn't grow up watching American television. "Never mind, you clearly wouldn't understand."

"Whatever, Hammer. Can we do this or not?"

I was carefully considering my options. I needed to keep Jackson and Emma safe until this shit with Boulder blew over. I'd learned recently Ray lived in the same apartment complex as Emma, which would make keeping an eye on both of them much easier.

"When do they arrive?"

"Saturday afternoon. Ray and I are picking them up from the airport."

"Fine, you can pick him up on Friday afternoon. He has an appointment—"

"I know he has an appointment. I'll just take him home from there."

Closing my eyes, I sent out a silent prayer this didn't blow up in my face. "I'll meet you at the clinic at two." Ending the call, I immediately dial my mother's number.

"I just heard from your sister. Is Emma okay?"

Stepping into the parking lot, I couldn't contain the smile which took over my face. Despite my mother's reservations about my decision to move forward with Emma, she'd embraced the idea of us together.

"She's signing the paperwork for Jackson now, which is why I called. I need you and Layla to scrounge up as many toys and clothes as you can for Jackson."

"The toys we got, but I will need to know Jackson's size first."

As I listened to the social worker discussing the temporary custody agreement, I'd learned Jackson and Liam were born three weeks apart. I was surprised to hear Emma list all of Jackson's favorite things, including the fast food she sent him and the clothes she'd mailed to the hotel where Macy was staying, all themed with his—and Liam's, favorite cartoon character.

"A size down from Liam, Ma. Get what you need, don't bother looking at price tags. Use the card I gave you. Listen, I know I dragged

you away from dad to watch Liam for me, but I just agreed to let him
stay with Kira while her future in-laws are in town."

"*Oh thank god. I'd forgotten about a meeting I need to attend and I was
racking my brain trying to find someone to watch him.*"

Movement from my left captured my attention. "Ma, I gotta go, see
you in a few." I ended the call, my heart tearing from my chest and
floating across the parking lot to Emma. She stood so confident, holding
an excited Jackson in her arms. I'd thought Emma was breathtakingly
beautiful when she'd first walked into the interview, somehow now she
was beyond measure.

"Ms. Shaw, I do hope you've remembered a car seat." I heard the
social worker say, bringing me back to the present.

"Of course we did," Hailey spoke through clenched teeth and I
wondered what happened in the time since I'd left. "It's in the trunk of
the car. I assumed you'd want to verify it was new."

Reaching into my pocket, I pressed the button to open the truck.

"Just following procedure, Counselor." The social worker retorted.

"No, you're being a bitch," I whispered to myself. I didn't know
who'd put the car seat in the trunk, but I suspected it was one of my
brothers.

"Excellent, Ms. Shaw." The social worker pushed her glasses up her
nose. "I feel comfortable letting you take Jason."

"Jackson." Emma corrected.

"Yes, well, have a good evening. Make sure to read over your respon-
sibilities as a caregiver."

"My client is well aware of what she signed," Hailey interrupted,
placing herself between Emma and the social worker. "Now, if you will
excuse us, we need to get *Jackson* home and fed."

I had to hold in the laugh as Hailey emphasized his name. I waited
until the social worker climbed into her car a few rows over before
making my way to them. We'd agreed I would remain in the shadows
while Emma and Hailey handled the paperwork. They were afraid this
situation may blur the lines of my own custody issue.

"Hey, big man," I cautiously approached Jackson. "My name is
Hammer and I hear you like chicken nuggets."

Big, soulful blue eyes met mine. His curly hair in a tossel around his cherub face. Jackson stared at me, clutching Emma's shirt with one hand while the thumb of the other disappeared into his mouth. He was thinner than Liam, and far shyer, but as Emma kissed his forehead, Jackson dropped the thumb from his mouth.

"With keth up."

Ketchup, Emma mouthed, although it was completely unnecessary. Since having Liam, I was well-versed in toddlerism.

"Me too," I exclaimed excitedly. "How about we go get some and take them to your Aunt Emma's house to eat?"

Jackson melted my heart as his eyes grew impossibly bigger, nodding his head as if it was his only job.

"Yes," I cheered, raising my hands above my head for emphasis. I didn't give a shit if I looked like an idiot, it made both Emma and Jackson smile.

"Where did all of this come from?" Emma whispered as the pair of us watched Jackson drag his tiny hand over the boxes of new toys.

Warden sent a text message while we were waiting in the line at the drive-thru. Keys had managed to live up to his road name by breaking into Emma's apartment and getting things ready for him

"It's what boyfriends do, babe." Placing my hand on the small of her back and rubbing what I hoped was comforting circles. "Besides, you're family."

Minutes after Warden's message, I received one from Ace, demanding my presence for a private meeting in the morning. I wasn't stupid enough to believe I could make such a bold statement to Emma and not have her father—whether biological or not—simply stand back without question. Despite Emma's attempts at separating herself from the Club, she was royalty.

"Titi?"

Jackson's excited voice pulled me back. According to Emma this was as close to 'auntie' as he could say.

"Look," he pointed at a box containing a battery operated motorcycle.

"I see it." Emma turned my way, the look in her eyes told me there was a conversation to be had once the baby was asleep. "How about we go have a bath and get into your new jammies? I bet Hammer will have the motorcycle ready for you to play with when we're done."

Jackson snapped his attention to me, rhythmically chewing the cookie the drive-thru worker gave him for being "too cute".

"Okay," he decided, crossing the room and handing me the half eaten cookie.

"Oh no," Emma reached for the soggy cookie. "Let me."

"Stop, sweetheart. You forget, I have Liam at home. This is the cleanest thing I've been handed in a while."

I could recall with perfect clarity the first time my son vomited in my hand. Kira had freaked out, but I'd simply wiped my hands on a blanket and cleaned him up.

"Weeum?" Jackson parroted.

Bending down, I put myself at his level. "Liam is my little boy. He's asleep right now, but you can play with him tomorrow."

Jackson surveyed me for several seconds before lifting his tiny hand to Emma. "Okay."

I watched as the pair walked down the short hallway into the bathroom. Listened as Jackson laughed while Emma tickled him while they waited for the tub to fill.

Making quick work of the box, I smiled as the song the pair sang drifted down the hall, the tenderness of it made me miss Liam.

I'd just finished plugging in the battery when Emma emerged from the hall. A hand-held monitor much like the one I used for Liam grasped in her hand.

"He's asleep," she whispered. Turning off the overhead lights and pointing at the loveseat against the far wall.

"Good," I stood to my full height. "Gives us a chance to talk about what happened earlier."

Stepping over the discarded box, I dropped my body onto the soft cushions. Emma hesitated a moment before joining me.

"I should have told you who I was from the beginning." She kept her head down, twisting the monitor round and round in her hands. "I'm sorry I deceived you."

"Why?" I questioned softly, taking a strand of her hair between my fingers.

"Ace said it best," she huffed. "I always choose my own path."

I could understand this. A few months before I'd patched in, I'd questioned if this life was what I wanted.

"I blamed Ace for my father's death, still do to an extent—since he was the man who'd sold him the drugs. He came in like a hero for my mother, letting her run the bar. Granted he was dealing his poison out the back, but he made her believe he loved her. Macy fell in step with the biker lifestyle, getting pregnant by Boulder when he was still a prospect. He made all these promises of them being a family when he'd jumped on his bike. The truth was, he'd found out he could challenge the president of Disciples, which, as you know, he did."

Dropping the strand of hair, I reached over and placed my finger under her chin, lifting her face toward me.

"You said Ace made your mother believe he loved her."

Emma nodded, but kept her gaze distant. "My mother once told me to fall for the guy who stood behind me and my dreams. The one who sees me for the woman I am and the one I'm capable of becoming. Most of all, he should treat me as if I were the most important thing in his life. Ace never did that for her. Granted, she never wanted for anything, but he broke her heart time and time again with all the women he paraded in front of her."

Sliding from the couch, I knelt in front of her, taking the monitor from her and placing it on the table behind me.

"You've seen how toxic the relationship between Kira and myself is?"

Emma searched my eyes, nodding silently.

"And if I know anything about her, you've likely heard how we played this twisted game with each other, inviting others into our bed."

Emma tucked her lips behind her teeth, closing her eyes as she nodded once again.

"What she didn't share with you, I'm sure, is during the times when we were together, I was one-hundred percent loyal to her. I didn't even look at another girl out of respect for her. Yes, it's true we invited other women into our bed, but it was done at her insistence, not mine. I was happy being in love with her. At least I thought it was love." Taking a measured breath, I ran my finger down her soft cheek. "Until I met you."

Emma's breath hitched, and I took it as a sign to continue. "When I said I was your boyfriend, I meant it. We can take this as slow or as fast as you want, so long as we're together."

Emma dropped her eyes down, a well of tears forming in the bottom. "You may want to take that back when you," she trailed off, a single tear falling down her cheek. "When you hear what I have to tell you."

Stilling my movements, I watched as a second tear trailed over my thumb.

"I've," she began, but stopped. "It's just," she stopped again, shaking her head and growing frustrated with herself.

"Hey," I gripped her face. "It's just you and me, sweetheart. Don't be afraid to tell me anything."

"I, um, I like the idea of you being my boyfriend. A lot actually."

"Good. So what's the problem?"

"You have a child, and have kissed numerous girls."

It began to piss me off when I heard Kira's hateful words flow from Emma's beautiful mouth.

"You're the perfect example of an alpha male and all it entails. While I sit here with my train wreck of a family, with an education that, up until a few days ago, I couldn't wait to use. For months, all I could think about was landing this dream job of mine, and now," she stopped abruptly, the corners of her lips turning into a frown as her sobs took over.

"Now, all I can think about is how disappointed you're going to be when I can't give you what you need. How If I follow my heart, you will undoubtedly shatter it when you figure out you can do so much better than me."

Moving to sit beside her, I wrapped her tightly in my arms. Rocking her gently, I waited until her sobs subsided before lifting her face up to mine.

"Few things, Emma. One, you having an education is a fucking turn

on for me. I want you to fulfill your dreams, living your life to its motherfucking fullest. I believe, when you make those who're most important
in your life happy, it comes back to you tenfold. As far as me shattering
your heart, I'd rather cut my own balls off than be the reason behind
your tears. I'm human, and I'm going to fuck up, but if you'll let me, I'll
make sure you never regret choosing me."

My heart expanded when Emma shared with me her watery smile.
Despite her red eyes and nose she was the most beautiful woman I'd
ever seen.

"I have so many emotions running around inside me right now I can
barely think. The last thing I want to do is make a decision when my
head isn't clear."

Nodding, I reached out and took her trembling hand in mine. I
understood what she's saying, and appreciated how level headed she
was despite the shit storm she's weathering.

"My feelings for you aren't going anywhere, if anything they've
grown stronger because of your honesty. When you're ready, I'm going
to claim what is mine."

Pulling her into my chest, I reclined us both as silence filled the room.
Holding her close, I kissed the top of her head, a battle plan formulating
inside my head. Emma was ruled by facts, she was calculated and careful, examining situations from every angle. I needed to prove to her I
was the best man for her. First, I had to convince Ace of that.

The cherry from Keys' cigarette glowed as he took a long drag. I'd called
him twenty minutes ago telling him I needed him to watch Emma's
apartment while I went to see Ace.

"How's she doing?" Tossing the cigarette to the ground and mashing
it with his boot.

"She's strong as fuck," I admitted, glancing across the parking lot at
the back of Ray's apartment. My gut had been screaming at me since I'd
learned he lived here. I couldn't put my finger on it, but something
was off.

"Everything okay, Hammer?" Keys followed my line of sight.

"I don't know yet. Keep an eye on Emma and Jackson."

"And Kira, too?"

Snapping my attention back to him. "You call me if that bitch even looks in this direction. Feel me?"

Emma didn't say it, but I knew she was worried about what would happen when Farrah and Kira find out who she is.

"I feel you, Hammer."

The smell of coffee hit me as I opened the Clubhouse door. Raiden and Bullet stood beside the bar with cups in hand.

"Well, he doesn't look freshly fucked."

Raising my middle finger in Raiden's direction, I headed for the coffee pot.

"That's because the beautiful Emma doesn't know what we do." Bullet mock whispered, causing me to stop mid-pour.

"The fuck are you talking about?"

"Boulder isn't pressing charges."

"How?" I stared at the pair through confused eyes.

"You tell him." Raiden pointed to Bullet, a cheshire smile on his face.

"No, you tell him." Bullet countered, contorting his face in a mock frown while shaking his free hand.

"I'll tell him," Ace's booming voice shattered the friendly banter. "Hammer and I have a few things to discuss anyway." He jerked his head to the left, a silent cue for me to follow him.

Filling my cup to the rim, I made my way toward him. Inside the room where we hold Church, I found Warden pacing in front of the window, his phone to his ear, listening intently to whoever was on the other line.

"Have a seat, Hammer. This won't take long."

"Why isn't Boulder pressing charges?" I rounded on him, my tone bordering on disrespectful.

Ace sat hard in the leather chair Warden normally occupied, letting out a heavy breath. "Boulder is guilty of many things, having a death wish isn't one of them." Ace took a measured sip of his coffee before continuing. "Macy stabbed him three times in his minuscule dick, enough to earn him three stitches and a tetanus shot. He refused to cooperate with authorities, leaving the hospital against medical advice."

"Leaving the DA without a case." I finished for him.

"Warden has been on the phone with your attorney for the past half hour, arranging for Macy's release."

My first thought was of Jackson. Macy was an admitted habitual drug user. Once out of jail, would she snatch him up and dive back into her lifestyle?

"Now Emma."

"I won't ask your permission to see her," I interrupted him, needing to establish my unwavering commitment from jump. "She's a grown woman and, despite her position in this Club, if we decided to have a relationship, it would be between us."

"You two are quite a pair," he laughed, leaning back in the chair and twisting it back and forth. "She won't make it easy for you, Hammer. I've known her since she was twelve, and she still harbors resentment for her father's death."

I remained silent. As much as I gave my loyalty to my brothers, I would give the same to Emma.

"It's easier to let her hate me than to tell her the truth about her father."

"Which is?" The question was out of my mouth before I could stop it.

"Darrin Shaw moved those girls from their home in Alabama because he owed someone a lot of money. He was a closet junkie, sniffing enough coke to keep him going, while he bounced from job to job. He got in deep with the wrong people and when they found him, they took what he owed. Sherry, her mother, told me the day they found him dead was the worst and best day of her life. She knew her husband's addiction was over. However, Emma was a daddy's girl, and it tore Sherry up to tell her daughter of his death."

"Who did he owe the money to?"

"No one you should worry about. I paid the debt a long time ago."

Fair enough, I thought to myself.

"Sorry about that," Warden sat hard in the seat beside me, his cell phone tumbling to the wooden table. "One call blended into two."

"Being the boss never stops, does it, Warden?"

Warden nodded his head slowly, but remained silent.

"Which is the original reason for my visit. Sherry reminded me a few months ago, we weren't getting any younger. She doesn't ask for much, so when she asked me to step down, I said I would. I've composed a short list of the men I feel could lead this Club and the two of you are in the top five."

"I'm sorry?"

"This has nothing to do with Emma. I'd made this decision before I knew she was here. Now, if you will excuse me, I've been away from Sherry longer than I'd planned."

Without a second thought, Ace stood to his feet and walked out the door.

"What the fuck? Did you know about this?"

Keeping his face down, Warden speared his fingers into the crown of his head. "I found out late last night. Roxie was entertaining a few of his men and they let it slip. Wanna know who he crossed off yesterday?"

Cocking my head to the side, I searched Warden's face when it hit me. "No," I drew out the word. Astonishment washed over my face as I watched Warden regretfully nod.

"Keep this to yourself. Let Ace be the one to tell him."

Leaning back in my chair, I took a healthy sip of my coffee. "I've got enough shit on my plate to worry about that bastard's problem."

"Speaking of problems," Warden reached for his phone, twisting it in his hand before shoving it into his pocket. "Farrah knows about Emma."

Emma

CHAPTER
NINETEEN
EMMA

"MORE, TITI."

Flipping the pancake I'd made for myself, I glanced at Jackson sitting at my kitchen table, a bib around his neck and a fork in his hand.

"Still hungry?" I shouldn't be surprised, he'd eaten all of his food last night and half of mine. He'd devoured four decent sized pancakes already this morning.

Reaching for his plate, I slide the fresh pancake onto the leftover syrup. "Here you go."

"Tank you," he mumbled around a bite, causing my heart to swell and my eyes to water. Turning to cook a pancake for myself, the sound of the doorbell halted my movements.

Glancing at the clock on the stove, "I wonder who that can be so early?" Hammer had left sometime in the night, not that I was surprised as I'd basically chased him off with my sobs and snotty nose.

Checking the peephole, I find Hailey standing on the other side of the door.

"What are you doing here so early? I thought you said court wouldn't start until nine."

Placing a kiss to my cheek, Hailey pushed past me, the same confidence in her step from last night. "If we still needed a judge, it would."

Spinning on my heels, my heart in my throat. "What do you mean? Is Macy okay?"

Hailey made her way to the kitchen table, taking a seat beside Jackson. "Boulder refused to press charges."

"How?"

Hailey's smile never faltered as she told me the story of his time in the emergency room.

"I've been in touch with the Club's contacts within the jail and they've assured me Macy's paperwork will be complete by the time we get there." Looking around the room at the stacks of toys and clothes. "Wow, Hammer doesn't do anything halfway, does he?"

Shifting my eyes to the motorcycle, my heart dropped at the thought Jackson may never get to ride it once he's back with Macy. "I hope he kept the receipts. Macy doesn't have anywhere for him to sleep, much less store toys."

Hailey insisted on cleaning up Jackson while I packed some clothing and toiletries for her. As I folded a pair of old sweats and a sweatshirt I'd acquired from the shop, I couldn't help but think of how different I was from my sister. She'd more than likely refuse the clothes, insisting she would rather wear the blood stained clothes she'd been arrested in. It's the thought that counts, I reminded myself, shoving a new toothbrush and paste into the grocery bag.

"Ready?" Reaching for my purse, I held out my hand to Jackson who shook his and buried his face into Hailey's skirt.

"He keeps saying Weeum."

Sharing a sad smile with Hailey, "That's toddler-ease for Liam. Hammer mentioned him last night before he left."

Bending down, I laid my hand on his shoulder. "We will go by Titi's work and see if Liam's dad is there."

"How about I go grab your sister and meet you two at the Club?"

Looking down at Jackson, his big blue eyes shining back at me. He deserved to have someone put him first for once. Handing the bag of clothes to Hailey. "Sounds great."

Opening the door, we were met by a smiling Keys, the smell of tobacco swirling around him.

"Hey, Little Man," he called to Jackson. "Where are you headed?"

"Titi work," Jackson proudly announced, jumping over a crack in the sidewalk. I'd let him pick his own outfit, giving him the opportunity to go through several bags.

"Jackson has yet to meet Liam," Hailey added, but my attention was across the parking lot and the three people standing by a running car.

Kira was leaning into the open driver's side window, her hand caressing the face of the man who'd given Jackson half of his DNA. The second man, a tall and much cleaner cut guy, stood beside Kira. I recognized him from the complex, but didn't know what his name was.

"Do you know that guy?" Keys spoke from my left, his phone raised as he snapped a photo.

"Not the one in the black jacket," I whispered, not that he could hear me.

"Best to keep your distance, Emma."

Keys' warning echoed inside my brain as I pulled into the gates of the Club. Was Kira a spy for the Club like Roxie? Surely Hammer wouldn't allow the mother of his child to be put in a place of such danger?

Something shifted in me when I saw Hammer walking from the Clubhouse, Liam high on his shoulders. He waved when he saw me pulling in, pointing at the parking spot not far from him.

"Hey, beautiful." Hammer placed a kiss on the corner of my mouth.

"Hey, bea ful," Liam mimicked, his kiss landing between my cheek and ear.

"Careful dude, that's my girl." Hammer teased Liam, flipping him off his shoulders, the toddler squealing with laughter.

"Titi!" Jackson shouted from the backseat, gaining both mine and Liam's attention.

"I'm here," I started, when Liam moved around my open door, climbing into the driver's seat and into the back to join Jackson.

"You'll get used to it," Hammer's arms wrapped around my stomach. "Liam is still fearless."

Turning my head to the left, I found Hammer's soulful eyes looking down on me. "Hi," my voice sounded breathy and full of lust

"I'm sorry I wasn't there to help you with Jackson this morning. I had a meeting with Ace."

Laying my hand on his forearm, "I don't expect you to insert yourself into my world."

Hammer shifted his attention to the back of the car, a smile tugging at his lips as he leaned into my side, nipping the lobe of my ear with his teeth. "I plan to insert myself into you over and over, sweetheart," he whispered, the huskiness of his voice making me shiver. "Come on, Sweetheart. Kannon called, he and Hailey are on their way with your sister." Hammer winked as he opened the back door of my car.

Reaching in, he growled at the two squealing toddlers as he unhooked Jackson from his car seat, telling them to go find Uncle Stoney for a snack. One of the prospects opened the door to the Clubhouse as soon as the tiny pair reached the building. He stood back as they shouted for Stoney, giving Hammer a thumbs up before closing the door.

Hearing the sound of a motor, I started to turn my head when Hammer pinned me to the side of the car, his lips covering mine in a hurried kiss. He didn't bother to ask permission as he pushed his tongue past my lips, wrapping it around mine. "I've wanted to taste you since I woke up beside you this morning." The deepness of his voice rendered me useless.

"Then why didn't you?"

"Because I gave you my word we would go at your pace."

"Says the man who just kissed my socks off."

A devilish grin commandeered Hammer's lips. "It wasn't your socks I was trying to get off." Leaning back, Hammer wagged his brows before stepping away.

The squealing of brakes pulled my gaze from Hammer's ass as he walked away to the mail jeep pulling alongside me.

"Morning, Emma." Jerry the mailman tipped his hat as he stepped onto the parking lot.

"Morning, Jerry." Puzzled as to why he didn't leave the mail in the box beside the main gate.

"Got a registered letter for you." He handed me the white envelope, the infamous green and white seal around the center. "Just need your signature," he added, handing me the signature pad.

Scribbling my name on the window before handing it back to him. "Thanks, Jerry, have a great day." I absently bade him as I took in the sender's name on the envelope.

A series of horn blasts pulled my attention from the envelope to the black SUV pulling into the drive, my sister waving from the back passenger side.

Kannon barely had time to put the SUV in park before Macy jumped from the seat and sprinted across the parking lot.

"Can we talk?"

Forcing the smile to remain on my face, "Of course. We can go into my office." Nodding my head toward the shop.

Macy looked to where I'd indicated, her brows furrowing in worry. "Is there somewhere more private?"

"What's going on, Macy?" I've seen this side of my sister one other time. The conversation centering around her needing a place to crash and resulting in me nearly losing my apartment.

Macy looked over her shoulder, following her line of sight, I saw Keys standing with his arms crossed over his chest, his attention on us.

"No," I shouted, gripping Macy's arm and dragging her into my office. "This is why I wouldn't let you know where I live." Slamming the door behind us, I crossed the room, closing the blinds to the shop and locking the door. "I need this job," I rounded on her. "What I don't need, is you fucking this up for me by sleeping with half the Club."

Macy tucked her hair behind her ears and lowered her head. "There was this woman, Paula, in the cell with me last night. She's much older than me, but the story of why she was in jail was the same as mine."

Lifting her face to mine, "Except the man she stabbed died. She said if she had to do it all again, she would have gotten her life together, never letting a man control who she was and what she did."

Leaning on the edge of my desk, I crossed my arms over my chest, but remained silent.

"I've let men control me my whole life, Emma. From Boulder to every guy in between. It's time I lived for myself, to be the kind of mom Jackson deserves. I want to go to rehab."

This wasn't the first time I'd heard this. "How much?" I deadpanned, knowing in the end Macy's problems always cost *me* money.

"Nothing."

"Really? You found a program for free from your jail cell?" She'd stayed two days in the last rehab facility I'd paid for. Deeming herself cured and checking herself out.

"I mean it isn't going to cost *you* anything," she emphasized.

Tilting my head to the side, "Then who? Because if you think—"

"Will you listen to me?" Macy interrupted, gripping my shoulders tightly and shaking me. "I don't need your help with money this time. I need you to keep Jackson."

Opening and closing my mouth like a fish, I tried to wrap my mind around how I could keep a toddler and still work. I had no clue how much daycare cost, but it couldn't come cheap.

"Of course I'll keep him, Macy. But where did you get the money?" I whispered the latter.

"Let's just say the ability to get a hard on isn't the only thing I took from Boulder."

"Macy," I chastised. "You can't steal from a guy like Boulder—"

"You don't know half of what he's taken from me," she seethed. "He owes me for the lies, the beatings, and for the addiction he pushed me into." Tears warred with anger as she purged herself of emotion I knew she'd kept bottled up for years.

"But mostly for the little boy he found so easy to toss away." Her voice cracked as she spoke the latter. I could count on one hand the number of times I'd witnessed my sister cry.

"So what's the plan?" I shifted the subject.

"I have a dental appointment this afternoon," Macy opened her mouth, pointing to her broken teeth. "Hailey got me in with her doctor and he thinks he can put a cap on them or something. Anyway, after that Keys offered to drive me to rehab. Some place his mother had some success with before she was sent to prison."

I made a mental note to ask Keys about this place when he returned.

"Sounds like you've got a solid plan."

"I do." She kissed my cheek, the excitement in her voice brought a smile to my lips. "But first, I need to say goodbye to Jackson."

Opening the door, I watched as she ran across the lot, knocking on the metal door of the clubhouse and waiting for someone to open it. Putting my fingers to my lips, I sent up a silent prayer that this time would work.

Closing the door, I made my way to my desk. I needed to find a daycare and fast. Tapping the spacebar of my keyboard, I caught sight of the registered letter from earlier. Reaching for a letter opener, I tore through the paper, pulling out the contents. Reading the words on the paper twice, my heart hovering in my throat as the door opened and Hammer walked in.

"Hey, babe," he faded off, the smile on his face shifting to concern. "What's wrong? Whose ass am I kicking?" He demanded as he cleared the distance from the door.

"No one's," I began, glancing at the date on the letter a second time. "I mean you can't," I shook my head. "This isn't—"

Snatching the letter from my hand, "The fuck I can't." His words were clipped as I watched his eyes dance as he read the letter.

"Motherfucking bastard!" He roared. "How can he still fuck with my life from the grave?"

Hammer

CHAPTER
TWENTY
HAMMER

WARDEN'S reaction was much like mine. He'd read the notice a dozen times before setting a series of f-bombs free.

"If I hadn't put the rope around that Angel bastard's neck myself, I would swear he was behind this."

I couldn't agree more with Warden. Angel de la Morte had managed to put everyone, with the exception of Keys, behind bars several years ago. He'd taken over the neighborhood and nearly crushed us. Leaning my chest against the wooden table, I reached for the bourbon I'd poured a minute ago. "Emma said sometimes it's random. A computer or some shit picks what the officials have to look at."

"I don't believe this is some random shit." Warden leaned back in his chair, sending the letter flying across the table. "Doesn't really matter, though. According to the notice, we have three days to respond or face a penalty."

Choosing to remain silent, my thoughts mirrored Warden's. We'd known for a while there was someone, or several someones, who wanted us gone. There'd been several attempts made against the Club, but they'd failed—until now.

With a heavy sigh, Warden stood to his full height. "If anyone needs me, I'll be in a meeting with the accountant."

Letting out a measured breath, "Uh, she's on—"

"Syn is not our accountant," Warden called over his shoulder. "We have a licensed, forensic accountant answering our motherfucking phones. Maybe it's time we use her to her full potential."

Jumping to my feet, I ran to catch up with him. Slowing my steps as he entered the furthest bay. "Shouldn't I be the one to ask her?"

"Nope," he clipped as we rounded the Honda Cisco is working on.

"Why not? She is my—"

"Because the letter is in my name, Hammer." Warden tilted his head back in exasperation. "Just like all of the utilities and insurance. Hell, even the trash is in my name." He didn't wait for a rebuttal from me as he pushed through the door and came to stand in front of a wide-eyed Emma.

"That IRS bullshit, can you handle it?"

"I, um, I can send a response to acknowledge receipt of the letter. However, I'd need access to the returns in question."

Warden pointed to the bank of file cabinets against the back wall. "They're in there."

I watched as Emma slowly turned in her chair, standing to her full height and crossing the room. She opened the first drawer she came to, flipping her thumb nail across the pages.

"There is no semblance of order, the years are intermingled." She mumbled, and I suspected it wasn't meant for our ears.

"Well, Emma, you get what you pay for. We've never had an issue with Syn doing the books. In hindsight, we should have gone with a professional."

I kept my lips sealed on how our original accountant met his untimely death when he was caught stealing. Syn filled in when we were in a pinch and we'd just kept her.

Emma opened a second drawer, pulling out several files before shoving them back. "If you're serious about me representing you during the audit, you'll have to find someone else to answer the phone."

"Done." Warden agreed, moving to leave.

"Hold on, I wasn't finished."

Crossing my arms over my chest, my dick twitching as I watched my girl taking control.

"The audit date is in fort-five days. I know from working with the IRS, I can get an additional sixty since I'm new to the case. Even with the extra time, I'll need a secure place to do this, a scanner, dedicated computer."

Warden waved his hand around, "Whatever you need."

"Oh, and one last thing," she held her finger up, taking measured steps back to her desk. "The salary you pay me is an entry level position. I have much higher rates as an accountant." Emma scribbled something on a piece of paper before handing it to Warden. "You can check my rate against anyone in town."

Handing me the piece of paper, I counted the number of zeros before looking into her beautiful face. Sending her a wink, "Done."

Lifting my leg to straddle my bike, I noticed Keys pulling into the lot. Snapping my helmet strap, he motioned for me to hold on.

"Did you get Macy settled?"

"It was a bit of a shock for her, but I think she's going to be okay."

When Kannon and Hailey came into the Clubhouse, they'd said Macy wanted a few minutes to talk with Emma about going to Knotty Pines Treatment Facility in the upper peninsula of Michigan. It was a hard core program where they lived off the land, no electricity or running water. Their success rate was off the charts, as was the cost to get in.

"I was hoping to catch you before you left."

"What's up?"

Keys reached into his pocket, pulling out his cell and handing it to me.

Glancing down, I looked at the grainy photo of Kira leaning into the driver's side window of Boulder's car, Ray standing next to her.

"Anyone else know about this?" Tapping the screen, I sent the photo to Warden and myself. The exchange could be completely innocent, but I highly doubted it.

"Emma saw them. I told her to stay away from them." My fingers stilled when I heard her name, a certain longing filling my chest. I'd never craved a woman like I did Emma.

"I'm going to need a favor." I handed him back his phone before pocketing my own.

"Name it."

"Emma is working on something for the Club and can't answer the phones anymore. I need you to grab a couple of the prospects and have them take turns."

"What about Lavender? She wanted the job before," he shrugged.

I could give him a million reasons why this would never work, but I chose to be simple and direct instead. "She also wants to ride my cock, neither one is happening."

Tilting his back in laughter, Keys pointed his index finger at me as he walked backward toward the office. I waited until he disappeared into the building before dialing my phone and raising it to my ear.

"Hey, you get the photo I sent you? Good, let's end this shit."

Emma

CHAPTER
TWENTY-ONE

EMMA

"AND SEND," I said out loud as I clicked the mouse, the swooshing sound of the email flying off to the internet filling the room. Glancing at the clock at the bottom of the screen, I was surprised to see I'd spent two hours writing the acknowledgment letter to Agent Frank Smith, informing him I would be representing Warden during the audit. I hadn't recognized the name, but it really didn't mean anything as the IRS had thousands of agents in their employ.

Leaning back in my chair, I took a hard look around the room filled with boxes. It had taken the team of prospects a little over an hour to pack all the drawers and haul them in here. Keys took a little longer finding the scanner I needed, but as I took it all in, I couldn't be happier.

I hadn't expected Warden and Hammer to accept the dollar amount I'd scribbled on the sheet of paper, but with the extra cash, I'd be able to pay for Jackson's daycare and rebuild my savings.

"Damn, the rumor is true."

Closing my eyes, I slowly turned toward the door, internally chastising myself for not locking it.

"Which rumor is that, Farrah? The one where you've lost your ability to speak? Oh wait, that was the wish I made."

Farrah swayed her hips as she walked into the room, running her fingers along the blinds covering the single window. Keys assured me no one used this room as not many knew about it.

"Funny," she wrinkled her nose before dusting her hands. "I was referencing the new job Warden gave you, despite the huge lie you told him."

"What lie?" I snapped, instantly regretting playing into her hands.

"The one where you conveniently left out you being biker royalty."

"Oh good lord, Farrah, I didn't lie. I don't consider Ace anything other than the guy my mother lives with." Turning back to my desk, I noticed the symbol for a new email at the bottom of my screen.

"Sweetheart, denying it doesn't make it go away."

Hovering the mouse over the new email, "Well, at least I got where I am because of what I've done, not who I am." Clicking on the email, I haphazardly glanced over the letter from Agent Smith confirming my credentials, as well as the time and place for the audit.

"What the fuck is that suppose to mean?"

Pushing away from my desk, "Oh come on, Farrah. I've heard about the fight you and Warden had in the parking lot." I pointed over my shoulder. "Where you accused him of being nothing without you. Truth is, you're the one who is nothing without this Club."

"My father—"

"There you go, Farrah, ride on daddy's coattails, cause we both know Warden isn't letting you ride on anything of his."

I'd seen the check Warden wrote to an attorney in Ann Arbor. My curiosity got the best of me so I googled the name and found him to be one of the best divorce lawyers in the state.

Farrah's eyes narrowed, "How dare you?"

"No, how dare you," I rounded the desk. "I have been nothing but respectful to you, even when you don't deserve it. Now, you come in here and accuse me of things which we both know are false."

"Don't think for a second who your father is changes who Hammer will choose in the end."

Shaking my head, I hook my hands on my hips, raising my face to the ceiling. "You know what, Farrah, my mother once told me; if he wants to, he will. I have neither the time nor the energy to discuss this anymore."

"This was my office," Farrah blurted, no doubt in a desperate attempt to unhinge me.

"And?" I deadpanned.

"Just seems par for the course, you get second hand everything. Ace's step daughter, Kira's husband, my office. Pity you can't have anything...new."

I was about to remind Farrah no one handed me my college education, but thought better of it. I'd never been one of those girls who needed to have the accomplishments in my life validated.

"Since this was once your office, I'm certain you know the way out." I returned instead, turning my attention back to my desk and the stack of receipts I'd begun sorting through.

"One more thing, Emma. I wouldn't get comfortable with the attention Hammer is shoving your way. He was born into this lifestyle and, as you are well aware, the rules of the road are different than when they're here. Road pussy is something all of them partake in, no matter who is waiting here at home."

I could see it in her eyes, a sliver of triumph that she'd cracked my shell. Hammer had shown up at my door early a few days ago, kissed my breath away before telling me he and a few other brother's had business they needed to handle. I knew better than to question what their business entailed. I'd returned his kiss and wished him a safe trip.

"Farrah, I'm surprised you don't have weeds growing out of your ass from all of the seeds of doubt you take such pleasure in planting. I'm well aware the rules of the road are different, but so is the man. Who are you to say Hammer will dive between the first set of thighs he comes across? Furthermore, it's none of your business if he does." I hadn't heard from Hammer since he'd left, which, until this moment, hadn't bothered me. "Now, if you'll excuse me, I have work to do."

Hours later, I heard the faint sound of classical music coming from the alley. The oddity of it stopped me in my tracks, forcing me from my chair and down the hall to the back door. Twisting the locks, I cringed as the door creaked with age as I pushed it open. Stepping into the fading light, I could hear the music and as I looked around, I noticed an extension cord plugged into an exterior socket, the end wedged between two slats in the fence where the music filtered.

"Thieving bastard," I growled, before reaching down and pulling the cord from the receptacle. The classical music abruptly ended as I tossed the end of the cord over the fence.

"What the heck is this?" I held up the faded receipt, squinting my eyes to read the amount. It had been like this for the past five days, one useless document after another. I placed the page into the growing stack I would review with Warden and Hammer, once they returned from wherever it was they'd run off to.

Glancing at my watch, I let out an exasperated breath as I realized I'd worked through lunch, again.

"Knock, knock," Kathleen peered around the corner of the door, her bright eyes making me miss Hammer even more. "I hate to interrupt."

"You're a welcome break, Kathleen. I've worked through lunch and I'm starving."

"Well, then I guess we can help each other."

"Oh?"

"Hammer asked me to pick up Liam from Kira's."

Several days ago, Hammer took Liam over to Kira's so she could introduce him to Ray's parents. Kathleen flew back to Florida and with everyone being so busy, I'd lost track of the days.

"He suggested I take you with me in case Kira was, well, Kira."

Standing to my full height, I dangled my sandwich in the air. "As long as you don't mind me eating this on the way."

Sliding into my car, I unwrapped a corner of my sandwich before taking a bite. Leaning into the buttery leather, I closed my eyes as I savored the sweetness of peanut butter and jelly.

"You know, we could grab some adult lunch before picking up Liam." Kathleen nodded toward my sandwich as I maneuvered around traffic.

"The joys of living with a toddler," I joked, tucking the sandwich into my purse.

"I'll have to take a raincheck for lunch, I have a lot of work to get done in a short period of time."

"Hammer mentioned the problem with the IRS." Shaking her head, as I signaled to turn into my complex. "Seems rather fishy to me, an audit during the time the boys were in jail."

I wanted to tell her how un-fishy this was, however, the sight at the end of the road captured my attention.

"Oh my god," my fingers flew to the gear shift as I slammed on the brakes.

"What?" Kathleen's voice faded as I jumped from the car, running across the parking lot. Dropping to my knees, "Hey, Liam." I spoke softly, holding my hand out to him.

"Emma?" His voice sounded hoarse, his face streaked with dried tears.

Reaching up, I made to remove my sweater, but Kathleen appeared at my left, draping a blanket around a naked Liam.

"Nana." The name was like a prayer as the tiny boy collapsed into her arms, his eyes closing as if in relief.

"That's right, Nana's got you."

Standing to my feet, dread filled my body as I approached the open door. Had something happened to Kira?

"Don't," Kathleen warned, her phone to her ear. "He has blood on his hands, I'm calling the police."

Hammer

CHAPTER
TWENTY-TWO
HAMMER

HOT WATER PELTED down my tired body from the shower head. Ducking my head into the spray, I closed my eyes, allowing the memory of the last kiss we'd shared to fill my memory. I'd hated leaving her so abruptly, but when Warden said jump, my response would always be how high. I could still taste her on my tongue, and longed to feel her soft skin under my fingertips. Emma was such a contradiction to Kira, there were no expectations or demands for anything. For the first time since I could recall, there was no dread in my chest as to whether or not a strange man slept in my bed.

"Quit jacking off, motherfucker. Warden is on the phone for you." Daxx pounded on the bathroom door.

Letting out a frustrated breath, I twisted off the water and threw back the curtain. Wrapping a towel around my waist, I jerked open the door to find a solemn looking Daxx sitting on the edge of the bed, my phone raised in his hand.

"Awe fuck." Fighting against the sense of urgency filling my chest, I crossed the room and snatched the phone from his hand.

"What's wrong?"

I listened as Warden told me how Emma and my mother found my son.

"Is he alright?" Spinning on my heels, I tossed the towel to the floor, sliding my legs into a clean pair of jeans. I needed to get the fuck home, now.

"He's as good as can be expected. Your mother said he ate two sandwiches and a plate of chicken nuggets Emma made him. The blood on his hands was his. The cop found a broken bong in the room where it appeared he'd been sleeping. Doc Ash looked at his fingers, but said the cuts were superficial. "

"Fucking Kira!" I roared, tossing my bag over my shoulder and heading for the door.

"That's not all."

Warden's tone stopped me in my tracks, my heart stalling as the bag in my grip slipped from my fingers.

"They found the items I sent you to look for in the closet."

Five days ago, a heated Kumarin called Warden demanding to know why he was missing a case of guns from the shipment SOC was hired to deliver. Our first thoughts went to Boulder, however Warden's plant denied his involvement. Bullet suggested our old friend Cash from Chicago, which is why I'd spent the last few days investigating his dismal Club.

"Why?" My words drifted off as I straddled my bike, Daxx following suit.

"Listen, I have eyes and ears out for Kira. Ray is on admin leave until the cops can investigate. Just get your ass back here as quickly as you can. Liam won't let Emma or Jackson leave, so everyone is camped out at your parents' condo."

Three hours later I cut the engine of my bike before running up the steps of my parents' condo. When Liam was born, my father purchased the place so they would have somewhere private to live during their stays.

Twisting the handle, the sound of laughter filled my ears, placing a calm in me I'd desperately needed. Rounding the first corner, I found Emma sleeping between Liam and Jackson, their attention fixed with the cartoon playing on the big screen.

"Daddy," Liam's gentle voice put a smile on my face. Crossing the room, I bent down and took him in my arms, the sweet smell of Emma's perfume filling my nose.

"Hey, Little Man." Holding him close, I looked down to see Emma's sleepy eyes looking back at me, the sadness there nearly buckling my knees.

"Ouchie," he whimpered, causing me to pull back. Liam held up his left hand with three fingers bandaged. "Kiss," he demanded, laying his digits against my lips.

Gripping his tiny hand, I covered his fingers with countless kisses, forcing a giggle from his little throat.

"Hey, Liam, how about we go get your daddy some of the cookies we made?" Emma held out her hands toward him.

"You made cookies?" My surprise was genuine, while my mother was incredible, she was no Betty Crocker.

"Emma did," my mother clarified, knowing me all too well. "You know me, that's what bakeries are for."

Handing Liam off to Emma, I waited until the three of them disappeared around the corner before snapping my attention to my mother.

"How much do you know?"

"Warden said you found him naked on the sidewalk."

"He was sitting in his own shit, Hammer," she clipped between clenched teeth. "Who knows how long he was there before we found him. Doc Ash said he'd lost five pounds."

My hands balled into fists at my side. I wanted to beat the shit out of Kira for being such a stupid cunt.

"There was no food in the house, and I'm guessing Warden told you what they found in the closet."

Nodding, I turned to the fireplace, leaning my arms on the painted wood.

"Kannon showed up with a social worker while the cops were doing their investigation. He wants you to call him as soon as you can."

Nodding, I pushed away from the mantel. "She told me Ray's parents were in town." Spearing my fingers into the top of my head. "I never would have left him with her if I—"

"Hey, this isn't your fault—"

"She's his mother, Mom. She's supposed to love him, not..." I trailed off when I heard the patter of little feet in the hall. "Not abandon him." I whispered as the trio walked into the room, Emma bent at the waist, holding a plate filled with cookies, the boys on either side trying to help.

"You made all of these?" Crossing the room, I took the plate, snatching a cookie from the top and shoving it into my mouth.

"Mmmm." Reaching for a second, I sat down on the couch, the boys joining me, each grabbing a cookie and taking a healthy bite. Liam burrowed into my side, his tiny fingers tracing the edge of one of my patches. Glancing up at Emma, I mouthed thank you, although I wanted to say so much more. Smiling her sweet smile, Emma crossed the room to sit beside Jackson, wrapping a protective arm around him as we collectively watched the movie still playing. As foreign as this felt, surrounded by toddlers and the two most important women in my life, there was no other place I'd rather be.

"I should go," Emma whispered as the credits rolled on the screen.

"Stay with me," I reached out, caressing the softness of her face.

"Not tonight," Emma looked at a sleeping Liam. "You need to be a dad more than you need to be a boyfriend."

This was the answer of a mom, one I both loved and hated. Wanting nothing more than to lose myself in her as I showed Emma what she meant to me.

"Lunch tomorrow?"

Nodding, Emma placed a gentle kiss on my lips. "Unless Warden fires me. I left for a quick lunch this afternoon and never returned."

Standing from the couch, I held my hand out for her. "Not a chance, darlin'. Now, let me walk you out."

Jackson slept soundly as I placed him in the car seat, closing the car door softly as I turned toward Emma.

"You sure I can't convince you to stay with me? I have a spare room." I pleaded, pulling her close and grinding my hardening cock into her hip.

"I'm not saying no." Her voice breathy as I scraped my teeth along the edge of her ear lobe. "Just not tonight."

Shifting my angle, I licked along the edge of her ear, nipping the skin of her neck as my hand slipped down her side, my fingers gathering the material of her dress. "You are so fucking incredible." I swore, dipping my fingers beyond the lace of her panties. "What you do to me?"

I sucked on the skin of her neck as my fingers slipped into her wetness. I wanted to consume her, feast on the essence which coated my fingers.

"Oh god," she purred, encouraging me to add a second finger and thumb to her clit.

"Hammer, we…we…"

"Shh, baby, just enjoy." I encouraged her before covering her lips with mine as I worked my fingers in and out of her. Dipping my tongue into her mouth, I captured hers with mine sucking in time with my fingers. I wanted this moment to last forever, and yet by the moans floating from Emma's throat and the way her walls spasmed around my fingers it was about to end.

"That's it, baby," I whispered against her lips as I increased the speed of my fingers. "Come for me." Flicking my thumb against her clit, I tightened my hold around her waist as she mumbled my name before collapsing against my chest.

"What was it you said about not being a boyfriend tonight?" I teased, removing my fingers from between her thighs and sliding them into my mouth.

"Hammer," she swatted at my chest, the look of shock on her face making me smile.

"Next time, I'm sampling from the source, without all of these clothes in my way."

Opening her car door, I helped her settle in, placing a not-so-chaste kiss to her lips before watching her back out of the space and disappear into the night.

I stood on the sidewalk, rocking back and forth on the balls of my boots, the scent of her still surrounding me. Pulling my phone from my pocket, I pressed the speed dial for Kannon as I took the steps two at a time.

"Hey, man, are you home?"

"Got back a few hours ago."

"*Good.*" Kannon drifted off and I knew something was wrong.

"What?"

"*We, um, found Kira.*"

Stilling my motions as I reached for the handle of the door. "Where?"

"*Chopper found her unconscious in an alley behind a house rented by Boulder.*"

"Where is she now?"

"*Paramedics took her to Detroit General when they couldn't revive her. I spoke with Doc Ash, she used her credentials as Kira's doctor to Baker Act her for a few days.*"

"Is three days enough time to get a judge to listen to my case?"

"*I'm going to pretend I didn't hear you ask me that.*"

"Whatever." Pushing the door open, Mom stood with her hands on her hips, eyes pinched in displeasure. "Call me when it's done." I barked before ending the call.

"Jonathan Alexander Sheppard."

"Awe fuck, Ma. Tonight is not—"

"Emma is not the kind of girl you pin to the side of a car, and disrespect like you did." She interrupted, jabbing her index finger into the center of my chest. "I'd suggest if you want to take her from an employee to my grandbaby's mother, you better treat her like a lady."

Dropping my gaze from her dagger filled eyes to the finger digging into my chest. "You're right, Ma, I'll apologize tomorrow. Right now, I'm taking my son and heading to bed."

Placing a kiss on my cheek, "I made up the guest room for you. Liam is already in his bed."

"Thanks, Ma." I called over my shoulder as I made my way down the hall. A devious smile coated my lips as I brought my fingers to my lips, savoring one last taste of Emma. "I'll apologize alright, by reminding her how good I can make her feel."

Emma

CHAPTER
TWENTY-THREE
EMMA

I INTENTIONALLY AVOIDED LOOKING across the parking lot at Ray and Kira's apartment as I pulled into my complex. As strange as it seemed, I was genuinely worried about Kira. Had she fallen into a bad situation, one which had taken her life? Or had she tossed motherhood behind her in some twisted and disgusting way?

Putting the car in park, I noticed a delivery man knocking on my neighbors door.

"Hey, is this you?" The man pointed at my neighbors door as I stepped from the car.

Shaking my head, "Sorry, she works crazy hours." I barely knew my elderly neighbor as she was never home.

"Can I leave these with you? I've got two more stops to make and my girlfriend is going to break up with me if I miss our date."

Pointing to the area between our apartments, "Leave it there and I'll take it in when I'm finished here." Tilting my head toward my car.

"Thank you, so much." The man put his hands together as if in prayer before disappearing into the back of the white van with June's Bloom's scrolled on the side.

I waited until the van pulled away before getting Jackson out of his booster seat. With Kira's disappearance fresh on my mind, I refused to take any chances.

Twisting the lock on my door, I fought hard not to stare at the three massive bouquets of roses sitting on the sidewalk. A sliver of jealousy pulled at my heart. I'd never received flowers for any reason, not even from Clark when we were dating.

I waited nearly an hour before I'd ventured out and grabbed the vases, leaving a note on my neighbors door to come see me when she got home.

As exhausting as the day had been, my mind refused to shut off. I'd assumed sleep would take me the second my head hit the pillow, but I'd been wrong. Guilt filled my chest as I thought of the hours I'd spent this afternoon not doing what I was paid to do. Then, if that wasn't bad enough, I worried if anyone had seen Hammer and I outside his mother's house.

"No one cares," I chastised myself, reaching for my laptop. This wasn't nineteen-forty after all, couples did much worse in far more visual places all the time.

Clicking on the accounting program, I snuggled in with my favorite thing in the world, numbers.

"Titi?"

Jackson's sleepy voice pulled me from my computer screen.

"Good morning," pulling him onto my lap. "Oh my goodness, those cookies are making you heavy." I pretended to groan as he curled himself into my arms.

"Cookies?" Jackson's head shot up, a look of excitement in his eyes.

"Nice try, handsome."

"I not handsome, I Jatson." Jackson protested, and I fought hard not to laugh.

"I'm so sorry," kissing his forehead. "Let's get you some breakfast and Titi more coffee."

Before I could move from the chair, my cell chirped with a new text. Glancing at the screen, I couldn't help but smile at seeing Hammer's name on the screen

> Do you have milk?

> I do.

> Good. Mom is out, Liam wants cereal and I want to kiss you.

> Then come over

I waited for him to reply, but the three dots never appeared at the bottom of my screen. Assuming he was driving, I moved to make more coffee when a knock sounded at my door.

"Weeum," Jackson cheered as he ran for the door.

"Hold on!" I shouted as I picked up Jackson and peeked out the security hole. A smile coated my lips as I saw Hammer standing on the other side.

"Hey, beautiful," he kissed my lips as he stepped over the threshold.

"Hey, fuful," Liam mimicked, sending me an air kiss over his father's shoulder.

"Good morning." Reaching out, I took Liam's tiny hand, placing a kiss to the back. "Who's ready for breakfast?" I questioned the room, as I made my way into my tiny kitchen. Sitting Jackson in his booster seat, I made my way to the cabinet, making two bowls of cereal and placing them in front of the boys.

"Want some coffee?" I called over my shoulder as I grabbed a mug for Hammer.

"Are you fucking him?"

Spinning around, "What?"

Hammer stood in the middle of my living room, pointing at the flowers on my coffee table.

"I said, are you fucking him?"

"No," I shake my head, "They—"

"Don't fucking lie to me!" He roared, causing Jackson to spill his cereal and start to cry.

Reaching for a towel, I wiped up the spilled milk as I took Jackson in my arms.

"I'm not lying." I say as calmly as I can, shushing Jackson who is hiding his face in my neck. "If—"

"Did you buy them?" He demanded, the tone of his voice making my anger rise.

"No."

"And I sure as shit didn't."

"I know," I tried again to reason, however the words which leave his lips steal any thought of an explanation.

"This is such bullshit!" He roared, pointing toward the innocent flowers. "Bitches don't get flowers for nothing," he added, I believe more to himself than me. "You had me so snowed, but you know what?" He pointed at me, a hatred in his eyes which shook me to my core. "You're no better than Kira, a hang-around, whore wanna-be."

Having lived with Ace during my teen years, I'd been privy to conversations of men about women who had little meaning to them. I'd gone out of my way to avoid the labels they'd placed on those women, the very words Hammer threw at me. I was none of those things, I knew this. Filling my lungs with a deep breath, I crossed the room, walking past Hammer to the front door. Letting the breath loose, I twisted the handle, pulled the door open and stood to the side.

"Get out," I instructed calmly, keeping my gaze on the wall opposite me and my free hand on Jackson's back.

"Answer me, dammit!"

"I said." Ignoring his demand, I squared my shoulders, "Get out."

"Not until you tell me his name."

Closing my eyes, I swallowed thickly as I turned my head in his direction. "In a little while, when you've had time to calm down and learn the truth, I might be willing to talk with you about this. This isn't that time and I want you to leave my house before I am forced to take further—"

"Call the fucking cops—" He interrupted, throwing his hands in the air.

"My call won't be to the police, Hammer. It will be," I trailed off, his name burning the tip of my tongue. "My father. I'm sure he'd love to know the colorful labels you have for his daughter."

Hammer stood stoically for several tense seconds before grabbing Liam and rushing out the door.

Hours later, I pulled Hammer's Mercedes into the lot after dropping Jackson off at daycare. Exiting the car, I walked into the garage bay.

"Cisco, are you here?"

The man in question walked around the corner, a rag in his hands and confusion in his eyes.

"Have the parts for my car arrived yet?"

Surprise replaced the confusion, his cheeks reddening as he silently nodded. "Hammer told me not to say anything."

Spinning on my heels, I typed my password into the computer. "It's fine, Cisco. How long did it take you to replace the part?"

Creating a new invoice, I'd known the cost of the part from the moment he'd ordered it.

"Two hours, maybe three." He shrugged as the sound of a motorcycle grew loud.

"I'm splitting the difference." I thought out loud, adding the cost of labor to the total. Pulling my credit card from my wallet, I scanned the plastic and signed the signature line.

"Can I have my keys, please?" Holding out my hand, as Cisco reached into the safe and handed them to me.

Movement in the parking lot caught my attention. Shifting my gaze, I caught Warden as he removed his helmet.

"Thanks," I told Cisco and hurried out of the bay, putting my keys in my purse.

"Hey, Emma, didn't expect you this early." Warden wagged his eyebrows. His expression fell when I didn't react.

"I need to talk to you."

"I heard about—"

"Not here, Warden, I need to keep this private." I interrupted, his head nodding in understanding.

"My office or yours?" His dark eyes boring into mine.

"Doesn't matter." My voice cracked, the walls I'd created earlier beginning to fall.

"Come on, sweetheart," he gripped my hand, tugging me toward the forbidden door.

"Coffee?" Warden pointed at the pot behind the bar. "Or does this conversation require something stronger?"

Crossing the small space to the bar, I leaned my arms on the polished surface. "Contrary to Hammer's recent belief, I'm not a big drinker," I spoke sarcastically.

Warden leaned against the bar, his eyes dancing between mine. "Awe hell," he swore before motioning for me to follow him.

Stepping into Warden's office, I dropped into the first chair I came to as Warden rounded the corner of his desk.

"Since you look as if you're about to cry and I don't give two shits as to Hammer's opinion of me," he reached into a drawer, pulling out a bottle of amber liquid. "I'm pouring us both a drink."

A single tear rolled down my face and I moved quickly to wipe it away. "I'm going to assume you're aware of what happened yesterday?" I hated how my voice was full of emotion, especially sitting across from a man who lacked any by nature.

"With Liam and Kira, you mean?" Warden slid the shot glass toward me. Tossing his back as he held my gaze.

"As someone who grew up, at least in part with this life, I know better than to expect you to take sides."

Leaning back in his seat, the leather groaned with his movements. Keeping his expression impassive, Warden remained silent as he waited for me to continue.

"Last night, I felt it important to allow Liam to have his father without anyone else vying for his attention. When I got home, there was a delivery driver," I faded off, my emotions nearly choking me.

Warden jumped to his feet and was around the desk in the blink of an eye, dropping to his knees before me. "Did this motherfucker hurt you?"

Shaking my head vigorously, "No. He was delivering flowers to my neighbor."

Warden surveyed my face before leaning against the edge of his desk.

Taking a deep breath, I told him the rest of the story, his eyes growing wide as I quoted Hammer's choice of words.

"Assuming you still want me to represent you, I'd like to begin working from home. Immediately."

Warden jumped to his feet, returning to the chair behind his desk. "Of course I want you to represent me. You're family—"

"There's something else I need from you." I interrupted, my heart racing as I considered my words carefully.

"Anything, Emma. If it's within my power."

Snapping my attention to the photo hanging on the wall behind him, two boys with toothless smiles and innocent eyes reflected back at me. The boy on the left was a much younger version of Warden, while the boy on the right was undoubtedly Hammer.

"Farrah said it best when she told me Hammer and Kira's relationship is unique. They seem to be attracted to one another based on the level of drama in their world."

Crossing his arms, Warden let out a humorous laugh, "Farrah is the original drama queen."

I could see on his face there was so much more to the story, however this conversation wasn't about him.

"Hammer needs to iron out the wrinkles in his life. As much as he would like to pretend he doesn't have feelings for Kira, her name is the first to cross his lips."

Warden nodded, "I can't argue with you there." Sitting up, he reached for my forgotten shot, silently asking my permission before tossing it down his throat.

"I have a few weeks left before the audit, I'd like for you to encourage him to work on himself during that time. As much as I need to be uninterrupted, he needs to learn how to fix his relationship with Kira, or how to let her go."

Warden speared his fingers through his hair, the dark strands slipping over his tan fingers like pieces of black silk.

"Hammer is like most alpha men, full of grit and rage. I've been guilty several times of allowing some of it slip out before my brain could overrule my tongue. While I'm not condoning what my VP said to you, I can't let you sit there thinking there's a snowball's chance in hell he'll ever want anything to do with Kira. That gash has betrayed him, and this Club, more times than any of us can count."

"Then why is she still here?" Slamming my eyes shut, I held up my hand. "Forget I asked—"

"No, you've been straight with me," Warden held up his hand. "I'm going to return the favor."

Balancing the heel of his boot on the edge of his desk, Warden leaned his chair back, tucking his hands behind his neck.

"After we learned of Kira's involvement with the Cartel, and her subsequent pregnancy, Farrah and several of the other ole' ladies came and pleaded Kira's case. They reminded me the child she carried was a Saint, deserving of all of the privileges provided under its umbrella. I used my position to order Hammer to learn how to co-parent, provide for his child and give Kira an opportunity to redeem herself."

"What happens if they can't find her?" The thought left my mouth of its own volition.

"You haven't heard?" Warden dropped his arms, tilting his head to the side. "They found Kira. She's now in the hands of medical professionals, where she will stay for the next few days. As far as Hammer, I will grant your request as long as you promise me one thing."

"Sure."

"I can't tell you what's about to happen, but your boy is about to go through some heavy shit. If you feel as if you can't forgive him, don't put him through the next six weeks of groveling—and trust me there will be plenty of groveling, be straight with him. If you need to break it off, do it now."

"Forgiving him isn't the issue, Warden. I could be a real witch and milk this for everything I can get."

"True," he bobbed his head.

"But I'm not Kira," I said with conviction. "I want a real relationship, not one based on obligation or boredom. He needs to want to be with me because I'll put us first, not because I'm good at starting an argument."

The sun was bright as I exited the Clubhouse, forcing me to shield my eyes as I made my way to my car. My vintage car was so different from the Mercedes, no soft seats or digital dashboard, and definitely no lingering scent of Hammer. Backing my car to the furthest bay, I unlocked the trunk and began loading as many boxes as I could fit into my car.

"Emma?" Keys' voice called down the hallway as I packed the files I'd left on my desk.

"In here," I called back, winding the cord of the scanner around my hand.

"Hey, I was hoping," Keys' smile faded with his words as he took in the state of my desk. "What's going on?"

"My situation has changed," I shrugged. "I'll be working from home from now on."

"Hammer didn't—"

"It wasn't his decision. Warden and I feel it's best considering the circumstances."

Keys nodded his head, but his eyes were full of confusion. "I, um, wanted to talk to you."

"So talk."

Keys blinked several times before beginning. "I've been exchanging letters with Macy. The rehab facility doesn't allow cell phones or computers, but they do let them receive letters."

Tucking the cord into an empty box, "I think that's nice." Macy could use a few friends in her life, especially once she comes out of rehab.

"I'd like to see her as more than a friend, eventually." I wasn't surprised in the least. My sister was a beautiful girl, with the ability to hold her own against guys like Keys.

"That's between the two of you."

"I know, but I'd like your blessing."

"She has a child," I reminded him. As much as I wanted Jackson to live with me forever, he was my sister's son.

Shrugging, "I was a child once."

"I'm serious, she comes with a lot of baggage. I need you to consider this before you slip your dick into her."

Keys helped me load the boxes into my car, swearing he would allow my sister to guide the relationship. As I turned toward the gate, I caught sight of Hammer coming through the entrance on his motorcycle. Our eyes locked as I passed him, raising my hand to wave, I mouthed the words. "Goodbye, Jonathan."

Hammer

CHAPTER
TWENTY-FOUR

HAMMER

"MY OFFICE, HAMMER."

I considered telling Warden to fuck off as I hung my helmet. My morning had consisted of one shit show after another thus far.

"If you're going to beat the shit out of me, might as well do it out here so we can hose off the blood."

"Oh, trust me, I wanted to make the beating I gave Bullet look like a school yard tiff. However, your girl robbed me of the pleasure."

Snapping my attention to Warden, "What the fuck?"

"Like I said, my office." He pointed toward the Clubhouse.

Dropping my body into the closest chair I came to, lulling my head back as the smell of Emma engulfed me.

"You know, I'd rather cut off my own balls than get involved with my brother's love life." Warden leaned on his forearms, and for the first time I noticed the discoloration under his eyes.

"You alright, man?" I pointed to my face.

Leaning back in his chair, "I have new neighbors who lack boundaries and the ability to answer their fucking door when I pound on it at four in the morning."

"I didn't know there were any homes available on your street." When

I'd learned where Emma lived, I'd contacted a realtor to find a house for rent on Warden and Bullet's street, but there weren't any.

"Behind me," he clarified.

The neighborhood behind Warden's had seen better days. Most of the homes were abandoned by their owners, too dilapidated to rent or sell. There were a few exceptions, but those were owned by young couples who'd taken advantage of the city's incentives to clean up Detroit. Definitely not a place I was willing to move Emma into, especially with Jackson in tow.

"Do I need to pay a visit?"

"Tell me something, Hammer," Warden leveled me with his gaze, ignoring my question. "When you were plotting the murder of the motherfucker who gave Emma flowers, did you bother to look at the card?"

Opening and closing my mouth, I glanced down at the two empty shot glasses on the desk.

"Emma was right," Warden snickered, dipping his head down before snapping it back to me. "You're so used to constantly having the worst thrown at you from Kira, you've forgotten who you were dealing with." Warden reached for a piece of paper, turning it over and sliding it toward me. "They were for her neighbor. An elderly woman by the name of Martha Allen, a birthday gift from her grandchildren. I confirmed it with the florist."

I stared at the grainy photo of three vases of roses lined along the sidewalk of Emma's apartment, the edge of her welcome mat in the corner.

Standing to my full height, I began to remove my Cut. I deserved to have the shit beaten out of me repeatedly until I got a fucking clue.

"Sit down, Hammer. Your punishment will be far more painful than my fist connecting to your jaw."

For the first time since I'd told Warden about Kira's involvement with the Cartel, I was nervous to receive his reaction.

"For the next seventy-two hours, you are to leave Emma alone. No dropping in on her, no phone calls or texts. Don't even think about using Liam as a loophole."

Swallowing thickly, my heart hovered in my throat so high it felt as if it were choking me. "Can—"

"Did you see me take a motherfucking breath? Give you a cunt-hair of a clue I was finished talking?" Warden slammed his hand on his desk, his face red with anger. "For years you've made excuse after excuse as to why you've kept Kira around. Hell, you've got me questioning which one of you is the girl in the relationship."

Clenching my jaw closed, I gripped the edge of the chair, anything to keep from launching myself across the desk at him.

"Emma isn't Kira."

"I know."

"No, you don't, so I will say it again. Emma isn't Kira." Warden emphasized the latter by pounding his fists against the desk.

"Look, I'm the last one to tell you about letting go of the past. I've had divorce papers in my desk drawer for weeks and haven't signed them. While I may suck at taking my own advice, I know my brothers. When Raiden lost his shit over Sissy, I made him take a break. Bullet needed his reset button pressed when he pulled his shit with Jillian."

Warden took a deep breath, his eyes drifting to the photos hanging on the wall. "You and I are so alike, Hammer. Too thick-headed to realize when to throw in the towel, and too proud to admit it."

Standing to his full height, Warden took several steps to the far wall, running his finger along the photo of him and Linx holding the trophy he'd won in a bike race.

"You have a chance at something great with Emma. Don't continue to be like me and toss away your dreams of the one thing you want most in life."

My leg bounced as I waited for the door at the far end of the hall to open. I'd been before a judge dozens of times, but this one made my stomach churn.

"Jonathan Sheppard." The bailiff's voice echoed against the marble walls.

"Come on, Hammer. Judge Fisher is as fair as they come." Hailey slapped me on the back, nudging me forward. The tie I'd purchased yesterday felt like a noose around my neck, the material of my suit making my skin itch.

I'd followed Warden's order, instead of driving to Emma's and begging for forgiveness, I'd shown up at Kannon's office where I dived head first into getting Kira out of both mine and Liam's lives. When Hailey brought in every piece of evidence we had of Kira's neglect, I'd come face to face with a reality I didn't like. Warden, and Emma by extension, were right in their accusations; I had made excuses for Kira's bad choices.

"Remember, unless he asks you a question directly, let me do the talking."

The sound of my dress shoes clicking against the tile added to the growing anxiety crawling inside my chest. Hailey reminded me at least a dozen times there would be no permanent decision made today. This was simply to get the ball rolling, to show the Family court severing Kira's parental rights was in Liam's best interests. The most we could hope for was a temporary custody order until the courts could review our evidence.

Stepping into the room, I was surprised to see the judge wasn't sitting on a platform, but behind a small desk in front of a large window.

"Please, take a seat." Judge Fisher extended his hand to the sofa facing him.

"Thank you, your Honor." Hailey spoke confidently as she walked into the room, as I trailed like a lost puppy behind her.

"I'd like to thank you for agreeing to hear Mr. Sheppard's case on such short notice."

I had no idea of what kind of back-room deals Hailey made to get this appointment. After I'd stared at the photos of Kira sucking Ángel de la Morte's dick, while Agent Hawthorne pounded into her ass, I questioned what in the fuck was wrong with me? I'd spent that evening playing with Liam and after he'd gone to sleep, I tried to think of one good memory I had of her. When I'd failed to remember more than a couple, I handed my phone and my keys to my ma before drinking half a bottle of Jack.

"Well, Counselor, your evidence was disturbing to say the least." Judge Fisher's eyes grew wide as he reached for the file with Liam's name on the edge.

Hailey had been a powerhouse, digging up photos and videos of Kira in one illegal activity after another. Arrest records and, with Daxx's help, pay stubs from Distractions.

"Is this the biological father of the minor in question?"

Judge Fisher reminded me of Santa Claus, with his white beard and hair, the readers poised on his nose only added to the look.

"Yes, your honor. You'll find the paternity test from a certified lab, along with a letter from the company detailing their identification process."

I'd been pissed about it at the time, not wanting to believe the baby she carried belonged to another man. Bullet had joked, saying it was better to be safe than sorry. I'd wanted to punch him at the time, now I owed the bastard a beer.

"I'm going to have to toss out the pay stubs. Work is work and I have no problems with parents doing whatever they legally can to support their children."

Hailey rocked back and forth on her heels. "Of course, your honor. The pay stubs were more to demonstrate the inconsistencies in her employment."

Judge Fisher looked to Hailey and then the pages in his hand. "Do we have pay stubs for Mr. Sheppard?" He questioned with a raised eyebrow.

"Yes, your honor. Mr. Sheppard is part owner of Inman Automotive. You should have his tax returns for the past five years."

I struggled to remain silent as the Judge placed Kira's pay stubs back into the file.

"Fine, I'll allow it."

I was focusing on breathing in and out instead of the way Judge Fisher perused the photographs. I wanted to tell him the stories behind each one, make him understand how much Kira had destroyed us. As he came to the final photo, the one of Liam sitting naked outside her apartment, my heart quickened as I heard him gasp before dropping the photo.

"Counselor, is this an open investigation?"

Hailey warned me about this. It was up to the Judge's discretion whether or not to use evidence in an open case.

"Yes, your Honor, by Child Protective Services and DPD, as one of their officer's is involved."

Judge Fisher remained unmoved, but kept the photograph in the file.

"And the mother? Has she been advised of this emergency session?"

This was the part I was most anxious over. Kira had been Baker Acted by Doc Ash. When she'd failed to wake up for the paramedics, she was given additional medication in the emergency room which made her slightly more lucid. Once she was in the psych ward, her condition deteriorated and the doctors were forced to move her to a medical floor. I was notified by the police she'd woken up on the morning of the third day, demanding I come and take her home. Hailey sent a process server instead and after tossing everything she could at the poor man, she checked herself out of the hospital AMA.

"She was, your honor. Although it was done during an inpatient stay in a local hospital."

Hailey said it was a fine line in the terminology for process serving. The statute made it clear they had to receive the notice at the last known address. Since she was inpatient, it was a gray area.

"I'm going to grant a temporary order with the following provisions. Ms. Sheppard—"

"We're not married," I interrupted, the words falling from my lips of their own volition. Glancing at a wide-eyed Hailey, I took a step forward. "I'm sorry, your honor. I've made more than my fair share of mistakes, but marrying Kira wasn't one of them."

Judge Fisher looked from me to Hailey, and then began chuckling. "Judging by all of this, it looks like you dodged a huge bullet."

Swiping his pen across several pages. "As I was saying, the mother will be served at her last place of residence, as I can't stand children being awarded to parents because of a technicality. You'll have a home visit from Child Services and we'll meet back in my office ten days from today."

Hailey waited until we were on the courthouse steps before she hit me with her briefcase. After she'd had her fill of punishing me, I wrapped her in a hug and thanked her.

"Come on, you owe me lunch."

Glancing at my phone, I saw it was well after twelve, and more importantly several hours past the seventy-two hours Warden had given me. Opening up my text app, I typed what I hoped would be the first step in repairing my relationship with Emma.

"Come on, Rocky. I'll take you to the closest gas station and buy you one of those frozen burritos."

Emma

CHAPTER
TWENTY-FIVE

EMMA

> I'm sorry for the terrible things I said to you. I don't deserve your forgiveness, but I want to try and make it up to you. I had good news today, and the only person I wanted to share it with was you.

I'D EXPECTED Hammer to chase me down the street. However, he'd stayed away. Warden let me know he'd had a serious talk with Hammer, one which had lit a fire in him.

> Thanks. I know you didn't mean them, doesn't make it hurt any less. I'm glad you have good news, maybe after the audit we could meet somewhere and talk.

Without interruptions, I'd managed to not only finish the audit, but review it three times, finding several errors in Warden's favor. I'd called Hailey to ask her to grab lunch with me to celebrate, but she said she was busy with an important case.

> I'd like that. Hopefully, I'll have even bigger news to share with you by then.

Erin called me the other morning, warning me Kira left the hospital and to keep an eye out for her. She'd had few details about Kira's health, but told me Liam had been in the clinic with Kathleen and told Doc Ash how much he missed his friend Jackson.

> I have to admit, you have me intrigued with this news of yours. Did you win the lottery?

I added dollar sign emojis to the text as a joke. I'd seen his bank account balance, and while I knew most of it was blood money, it was enough to widen the eye of any philanthropist.

> I don't mean to tease you, and I promise the wait will be worth it. Tell me, Emma. What would you buy if you won the lottery?

I didn't have to think about my answer, yet I couldn't type it fast enough.

> If I were to win the lottery, I'd open my own accounting firm. One where I could help others, like I'm helping Warden use the IRS rules against them.

I'd printed out every statute, triple checked the wording and made sure I had the correct forms completed. I'd received several emails from Mr. Smith outlining the penalties he was prepared to issue. His last correspondence was an offer to issue the penalties and if paid in full, he would cancel the audit. I'd advised Warden this was highly unusual and showed him the errors in his favor I found. He'd told me to not-so-politely decline, but I'd chosen to remain professional in my response.

> Wait, I thought you said you wanted to work for the IRS. Did something change?

Taking a huge breath, I leaned back in my chair. So much had changed since I'd come to work for SOC. In the six months since I'd walked in the front door, I'd become so much stronger. No longer afraid of the parts of my past I couldn't change.

> So many things have changed, I don't think I will ever have enough space to list them. I used to think I had my life planned out, this safe existence with a man who would make all of my dreams come true.

> I'm sorry I shattered them.

> You're assuming I was referring to you.

The retort was on the screen before I could think about it. Hammer had hurt my feelings, and he needed to decide who he wanted to be with.

> No assumption, sweetheart. The difference between Clark and I, is I'm trying to make things right. Even if the only thing you allow me to be is your friend, I will fulfill that role with the same loyalty I did when I was your boyfriend.

I read and reread the last part of his text, my heart pounding against my chest with anxiety.

I take it you've made your decision. I typed, but slowly deleted it. I hadn't considered us broken up, but it was clear he did.

> Your loyalty is one of your best qualities.

I typed instead, adding a smiley face emoji. Tossing my phone to the comforter, I switched off the lamp and pulled the blanket under my chin.

I checked the address on the letter three times as I looked at the nondescript building. Glancing around, a sense of unease filled my chest as I took in the neighborhood.

"Ms. Shaw?"

Startled, I let out a scream as I turned toward the voice. Standing in the open doorway was a red haired woman with black rimmed glasses.

"I'm so sorry, I saw you standing out here. You are, Ms. Shaw, correct?" She pointed a perfectly manicured finger at me.

"Yes, sorry." I adjusted the strap on my shoulder. "I thought I had the wrong address."

Opening the door wider, it didn't escape me the woman failed to introduce herself.

"What can I say?" She shrugged, stepping into the dark space. "Budget cuts at their finest."

Following her lead, I stepped over the threshold, a chill running down my spine as I took in the simple room. A single desk sat in the center of the room, a lonely monitor with a cup filled with pens resting on top.

"Mr. Smith is waiting for you," she pointed to the half-open door on the far wall. "Can I hold anything for you?"

Donning the smile I reserved for Ace. "Are you kidding? This is downtown Detroit, I didn't even wear my good panties."

Stepping around the redhead, I made my way to the back of the room, knocking softly on the open door.

"Hello?"

"Awe, Ms. Shaw, I presume?" A man dressed in a black suit and purple tie stood from the table. His accent was thick with a northern dialect and his features were sharp.

"Pleasure to meet you, Mr. Smith." I extended my hand, covertly looking for his identification badge. Movement from my left caused me to look to the far corner, I had to work overtime to maintain my smile.

"Allow me to introduce you to my boss, Mr. Anderson." Smith let go of my hand and pointed to the man in the corner. "It's time for my annual evaluation and since this audit was already scheduled."

"Of course, kill two birds with one stone." I chuckled, purposely avoiding shaking hands with Mr. Anderson. "Shall we get started?" I pointed to the desk with a stack of manilla folders on it.

"Please, take a seat." Frank waved in the direction of the table.

Taking the single seat, I tucked my briefcase on my lap, rubbing my index fingers against the bracelet on my wrist.

"I'll begin by offering the penalties again. I'm assuming you brought a check from your client with you." Frank smiled, pointing to my lap.

"As per my last email, we respectfully decline option one and would like to proceed with the official audit." Purposely avoiding his question.

"Alright," Frank leaned back in his chair, reaching for the file on the top of the stack.

"According to the return filed by your client, Mr. Warden." Frank slid a form 2072 toward me, "He claimed to have earned less than thirty-thousand dollars, when the previous year was substantially more. Care to explain?"

Lifting my gaze from the form to Frank's dark eyes, "Care to show me your badge?"

"You'll have to forgive me, Ms. Shaw, I left my badge at home today."

"Your CAC card will suffice." I countered.

"At home on my kitchen counter I'm afraid." Frank smiled, the lie slipping from his tongue like spun silk.

Picking up the form from the table, I locked eyes with Frank, taking the corners between my fingers. "Well, *Frank*," I emphasized his name. "Form 2072 hasn't been used since the Reagan era. As far as your CAC card, you wouldn't have been able to access any of your systems without it." Ripping the page slowly in half.

Frank leaned back in his chair, folding his arms over his chest, causing a sliver of a tattoo to be revealed. There wasn't a lot of ink showing, but just like the man in the corner, it looked oddly familiar..

"You should be careful, little girl."

Reaching over, I grabbed the skin of his arm, pinching the ink there. "No. You should have done your homework before trying to con the wrong company."

Frank ripped his arm away from me as the man in the corner let out a laugh. "You think you're here so we can con you?"

"I don't know, Colby. How about you fill me in?" I deadpanned.

"Last motherfucker to call me that—" He began, but I cut him off.

"Save me your dramatics, dude, and tell me why I'm here."

I'd heard stories of Boom and how he'd run his mouth about taking over for Ace. Back peddling like a little punk when Ace confronted him.

"I have a message for you to give to your boss."

"You mean Mr. Warden?" I snapped back, making my voice a few octaves higher mocking him.

"I could slit your throat," Boom jumped to his feet.

"But then you'd have to answer to my father." I held up my right hand, the bracelet dangling from it. "You remember him, Colby? Ace Mackenzie?"

"Nice try, bitch." Boom laughed, twisting the metal chair and straddling it. "Ace has one daughter and you ain't her."

"There you go slacking on your homework again, he has two. My sister, who you've met, and me, the one who avoided bikers like the plague." I sneered. I may have zero appreciation for my step-father, but I did pay attention when he spoke. Ace taught me how to stare down a bully, finding their weak spot and capitalizing on it.

Colby studied me for the longest time, his heavy gaze making my skin crawl. "Tell Warden he has a rat in his ranks."

"Spoken like a man of experience," I challenged, a knowing smirk on my face. Boom had shown up on one of Ace's Open Gate nights. At first he was a go-getter, but Ace was never one to trust easily. When Boom was caught red-handed stealing money from the Club, it was the final straw for Ace. Boom was beaten and left for dead. Last I'd heard he'd joined up with a group of skinheads, however judging by the Cut on his shoulders, he'd found a new Club to accept him.

"If Warden knows what's good for him, he'll stop moving guns in Disciples territory"

Reaching into my briefcase, I pulled out the envelope I'd tucked there earlier. "I was asked to give this to you." Holding out the envelope, I stood to my full height and tossed the white square into Boom's chest. "I'll see myself out," I called over my shoulder, catching the shocked look on Boom's face as I waved goodbye to the redhead.

Hammer

CHAPTER
TWENTY-SIX
HAMMER

> Come see me when you're done with court.

I SMILED as I read the text from Warden. Today was the IRS audit and I suspected he was anxious about the outcome.

> Miss me already?

> Hardly. Emma brought a message back from the IRS.

While I found his choice of words odd, I didn't question it. Reading her name, I flipped to the conversation I'd been having with her. I'd wished her good luck early this morning, but according to my phone, she'd yet to read it. Scrolling to the beginning of the conversation, I recalled how I'd chosen my words carefully, baby steps I'd reminded myself. My stomach dropped when I reread a portion of the conversation where it appeared I'd referenced myself as her former boyfriend.

> Hey, beautiful. I just realized I previously referred to myself in the past tense on being your boyfriend. Nothing could be further from the truth. I am, and will always be...yours.

"Jonathan Sheppard," the bailiff called down the hall. A sense of deja vu surrounding me. Pocketing my phone, I followed Hailey down the corridor, focusing on the click of her heels instead of my racing heart.

Inside the room was the same with the exception of Gloria, the Child Protective Services officer who'd visited mine and my mother's house the other day, sitting in a chair in the corner of the room.

Judge Fisher sat with his hands tented, the glasses he wore last time resting atop a leather bound book.

"Counselor, we are going to give Ms. Rogers a few more minutes."

"Of course, your honor. I heard there was an accident on seventy-five."

Shifting my attention to the clock on the wall, I watched as the second hand spun around the face countless times until Judge Fisher called the hearing to order.

I listened as the Judge asked Gloria about the condition of my home, how much food was in my refrigerator and if she had any concerns. Keeping my body still I silently celebrated when Gloria boasted of how meticulous my house was. I had Daxx to thank for that, having called him on the way home from the emergency session, I gave him free reign to organize away.

"In the thirty years I've been with the department, I've never seen such a well-adjusted child. The only concern I have is asking Mr. Sheppard who Jackson is?"

I waited until the judge looked at me, motioning with his hands for me to answer. "Jackson is my girlfriend's nephew. They are close in age and circumstances, as Jackson's mother is also dealing with an addiction."

Gloria smiled and then made a note on a packet of paper in front of her. "Thank you, Mr. Sheppard. Liam made it seem as if he were a sibling."

A mental picture of Emma swollen with my child flashed in my mind's eye. One pregnancy with Kira had been a bad enough ordeal to swear me off from any children in the future. With Emma, I was definitely rethinking my decision.

"I've read the reports and spoken with both the psychologist and

Liam's pediatrician. Based on the evidence presented, and in light of Ms. Rogers' failure to appear before this court, I am revoking her parental rights, effective immediately."

Judge Fisher scribbled his signature at the bottom of the page, stamping his seal on the edge before turning to me.

"Mr. Sheppard, I want you to know, I do not take pleasure in separating parents from their children, especially mothers. In this case, I have no doubt I've made the right decision. I wish you good luck in raising Liam."

Standing from my chair, I crossed the small space and held out my hand. "It wasn't easy coming here and asking to have Kira removed from Liam's life. Maybe now we can both live a better, less toxic, life."

Hailey waited until we were in the car before raising her hands in the air and letting out an ear-numbing scream.

"We did it, Hammer. We won our case."

"You won our case," I corrected her, rolling down the window and paying the parking attendant.

"I have to call Emma. See how her audit went and if she wants to celebrate with me."

Pulling into traffic, I headed toward Kannon's office. I'd given him my word I would return his girl in the same condition I took her in. Thankfully his office was only a few blocks from the court house. I forced myself to ignore her conversation. I couldn't wait to tell Emma I'd severed the last tie to Kira.

"Dang it, voicemail." Hailey swore as she waited for Emma's greeting to finish. "Hey, Emma, it's Hailey. Listen, I know this is last minute and all, but I was wondering if you'd meet me for dinner tonight as I have something to celebrate and I'm certain you do too. Kannon has a deposition and Hammer has Church. Call me when you get this, okay? Love you, bye."

Hailey tapped the screen and shoved her phone into her briefcase.

"How do you know I have Church tonight?"

"Because I'm an SOC attorney, Warden added me to the text."

Tossing my tie to the seat of my Mercedes, I made my way into the Clubhouse.

"Hey man, how did it go?" Daxx stood behind the bar pouring a beer.

"Kira didn't show, so the judge granted our petition."

Raiden's eyes widened, "Are you serious? After everything you did, she didn't bother to show?"

Rolling up the sleeves of my dress shirt. "Kira was never mother material. I'm glad it happened now instead of years down the road when he'll remember."

Daxx pointed to the tap, silently asking if I'd like a beer.

"A beer sounds great." Glancing around the room. "Hey, where's your dad?"

Raiden and Daxx shared a look. "Stoney took Syn to her doctor's appointment. He called a little while ago and said they were going to the hospital for a stress test."

Taking a long pull of my beer, "Kira had a few of those, granted she was doing God knows what at the time."

Raiden raised his glass, "A toast."

"Bring a couple of pitchers, Raiden. We're gonna need them." Warden ordered as his boots ate up the distance in the room. Daxx sent me a worried look before turning around and grabbing several pitchers.

Following Warden into the room, I rounded the table and took my place beside him. "Did something happen while I was in court?"

Warden took a deep breath before tossing his phone onto the table. Turning his face toward mine, "I need you to trust me."

Squinting my eyes, I mimicked his stare. "Don't I usually?"

"Yes, Hammer, you do. But this time is different."

The seriousness of his words gave me pause. Searching his face, before I could question what he'd meant, Daxx set the beer in the center of the table.

I nervously watched as Warden looked around the table before pointing at Keys. "Where's Chopper?"

Keys lifted his gaze from his phone. "Helping Raiden carry in glasses."

The sound of clinking glass preceded Chopper and Raiden walking into the room, each with a tray filled with frosted glasses.

"Chopper, have a seat," Warden slammed his hand on the table beside him.

Warden motioned for Daxx to fill the glasses, taking the first full one and placing it in front of Chopper. Taking a second glass, Warden held it high in the air. "I was skeptical when you first came to us and wanted to help us deal with Boom." Reaching over, Warden clinked his glass with Chopper's. "Thanks for feeding your brother enough bullshit he actually thinks he stands a chance against us."

Daxx slid a glass in front of me, before taking a healthy swig from his own.

"And, Hammer, wait until you see your girl. Man, she handled Boom like a fucking boss." Warden smiled as he leaned into me.

Pride and longing warred with each other inside my chest. It had taken a lot of negotiations on Warden's part before I'd agreed to allow Emma to go to the meeting. It wasn't until I'd met the man who would be watching her from the rooftop across the street that I'd agreed to Warden's plan.

"I hate to break this up," Raiden held up his cell phone, placing his nearly empty glass on the table. "We have a new member of the SOC family. Syn had a baby boy."

Emma

CHAPTER
TWENTY-SEVEN

EMMA

TUGGING at the hem of my dress, I stared at the woman in the mirror. I'd never been one to wear revealing clothing, even during the heat of the summer. I preferred a dress below my knees to the cheek-showing shorts Macy wore.

"Holy shit, girl. Where have you been hiding those legs?" Erin's smiling face appeared beside my more solemn one. Her excitement caught the attention of the group and before I could blink everyone was staring at me.

Jillian cleared the distance, wrapping a comforting arm around me. "Don't listen to it," she whispered, keeping our eyes locked in the mirror. "That little voice inside your head telling you this dress makes you look anything other than smoking hot."

I wasn't sure how she'd known, but I also wasn't ready to spill my past into the waiting ears of a bunch of girls I barely knew.

"Just not used to anything this short." I smiled, hoping she couldn't feel the shakiness in my limbs.

"Are we ready?" An excited Hailey bounced into the bedroom. Warden begged me to take Hailey up on her invitation to celebrate, and had me swearing not to say anything about Boom being in town. I'd bargained the story of Boom's obsession with Hailey out of him, connecting the dots to the half-story Roxie shared the day they took me to lunch. I'd tried to argue I had no one to watch Jackson, however Erin stepped in saying Drew, Doc Ash's husband, had been pestering her to have more children. She wanted him to see what having four children under the age of five was like. Once Jackson had learned Liam would be there, I couldn't move fast enough to get him to Doc Ash's.

"Ready?" Erin questioned, her smile boosting my courage.

"Absolutely," I agreed, tugging on my hem one last time before joining the other girls.

"Hello, ladies. My name is Caesar and I'll be your waiter this evening."

An hour after we'd left, we were seated at a table overlooking the city at the infamous Oak Room, our reservation was compliments of Drew Kumarin who'd insisted the celebration was on him.

"Are we celebrating anything special this evening?" Caesar circled the table with his kind eyes.

"As a matter of fact, we are, Caesar." Hailey pointed at herself, "I won a case for an important client." Nodding her head to the left, "She aced her last final of the semester." Erin waved, the proud smile on her face contagious. I'd learned on the way over Erin was in medical school, something Raiden—and the Club by extension, supported.

"This one over here picked a wedding date," Jillian nodded, wiggling the hand which housed the massive diamond Bullet put there.

"And this gorgeous woman took on the IRS and won." A pang of guilt hit me in the chest as the pride in her words came raining down on me. The feeling of something off flooded me after receiving the email from Agent Smith. Studying the IP address, I made a call to Warden who asked to have the email forwarded to him. Several days later, Warden came to my office, showed me the IP trail he'd done. The street address of the sender belonging to one of the properties owned by Disciples of Destruction. I assumed he would want to cancel the alleged audit, however, when he laid out his plan, I couldn't help but readily agree. He'd sworn my safety, and made me promise to keep the plan a secret.

"Oh my, this calls for champagne," Caesar exclaimed, spinning on his heels and disappearing before we could protest.

"To doing what you love," Hailey held a champagne glass high in the air.

"And looking fantastic while you do it, "Jillian added while pointing her glass in my direction.

I tentatively raised the glass to my lips, the bubbles tickling my nose.

"Hey, don't look now, but that guy over there is totally checking you out." Erin leaned across the table, her attempted whisper a little louder due to the champagne.

"What guy?" Jillian searched the room. "I wanna see him before Hammer wipes the floor with him."

"Hammer isn't here," I reminded her.

"Oh, sweetheart, just because you can't see him, doesn't mean he isn't here."

I wanted to remind her Hammer and I hadn't seen one another in weeks, however as I followed where Erin continued to stare. My heart skipped a beat when I saw the man in question.

"Excuse me," I tossed my napkin to the table as I jumped from my chair. I watched as the smile on his face morphed from interested to bewildered, and finally, moments before I stood before him, stunned.

"Emma?"

"Clark."

"What are you doing here?

"I'm celebrating with my friends." I turned slightly, motioning to the table I'd left behind. "What about you?"

"It's my sister's birthday."

"Oh?" Looking around the restaurant, "Where is she?"

"You missed her," he snickered. "She's expecting another baby and the celebration tired her out." His expression sobered, "I tried to call you, after what happened at my father's retirement."

"Why?"

Clark dropped his gaze to the leather of his polished shoes, rocking back and forth on the balls of his feet. "My father insisted I apologize to you,"

"Okay," I drew out the word as I waited for the punchline. "So apologize."

Clark lifted his head back in laughter, gaining the attention of a couple of women returning from the bathroom to our left.

"Haven't you heard? My father sold the firm. I've had to seek," he stopped abruptly, casting a worried look around the room. "A less desirable source of employment."

Everything in me wanted to jump down the rabbit hole and ask him what he'd meant by his choice of words. However, as I looked at the man who I'd once thought was my forever, I found myself asking what I'd ever found attractive in him? Had I been so desperate to separate myself from the life I'd left, I was willing to take the first man to show me any attention?

"Interesting choice in attire, Emma," Clark pointed toward my dress. "Not something I've ever seen you wear."

"Is there something wrong with my dress?" I couldn't argue with him, historically I'd been on the extreme side of conservative.

Clark snickered before taking a drink from the glass in his hand, "Come on, Emma. You know you don't have what it takes to pull this look off."

And there it was. The sharp tongue which cut like a knife, severing the confidence I'd worked so hard to build. Clark's words to me had bordered on cruel and for years I'd made excuses, attributed the slashes he took at me as side effects of his numerous medications.

"Who's your friend, sweetheart?"

Snapping my head to the side, a sense of relief washed over me as I took in Kannon's concerned face. Ignoring the possible repercussions, I melted into his touch.

"Don't I know you?" Clark looked at Kannon, a bewildered expression on his face.

"I doubt it," Kannon placed his hand in the center of my back, rubbing comforting circles there. "Unless you frequent the local jail or courthouse."

Kannon pulled me closer, "You ready to get out of here?"

Gratitude washed over me as Kannon didn't seem to care to listen to Clark's answer. "Yes."

Wrapping my hand around Kannon's arm, I took a step before Clark gripped my free hand.

"Hold on, Emma."

In the blink of an eye, Kannon slid his body between mine and Clark's.

"Take your hand off her."

Kannon towered over Clark, his voice deep and threatening.

"I was—"

"I won't repeat myself," Kannon warned, interrupting Clark who dropped his hand as if my arm were a hot poker.

"Come on, Emma," Keys whispered in my ear, as he took my hand and began leading me away from the two. "Let's get you out of here."

Keys tucked me under his chin as he escorted me to the elevator. As the floors ticked by, my mind flashed back to the words Clark used. Was he right? Did I lack something to pull off a piece of clothing, and by extension, the look of appreciation?

"The girls are waiting in the car—" Keys began, but as the final two floors rushed by, a thought slammed into my mind.

Stepping into the garage, I waved at the waiting car. "You guys have fun, I'm not ready to call it a night." Three sets of bewildered eyes stared back at me as I reached for my cell. "I'm going to call a car service."

"The hell you are," Keys snatched the phone from my fingers. "Where do you want to go?"

Half an hour later, I stood on a stone porch, my hand raised to push the doorbell. Glancing over my shoulder, I waved to Keys as he backed out of the driveway.

Stealing my breath, I leaned forward to press the button when the wooden door flew open to reveal a shirtless Hammer.

"Emma?" Hammer's deep voice was almost enough to rob my attention from his bare chest. Smooth skin stretched over toned muscle, a colorful collage of inked designs blanketed his left side.

It was the booming sound of Keys' engine which pushed me out of my fantasy tour of his chest.

"I'm sorry," the apology was out of my mouth of its own volition. "I didn't...I mean...I shouldn't." Stuttering over my words, I closed my eyes and took a measured breath.

"Want to come in?" Opening the door wider, Hammer stepped to the side, waving his arm in invitation.

Stepping over the threshold, I was shocked to see how well decorated his home is. A black leather sectional sat opposite a fireplace with a television hanging above. Various framed photographs of Liam stood on a console table against a far wall, a miniature motorcycle resting against one of the legs.

"Can I get—"

"Can I pull off this dress?"

A smile tickled at the edge of Hammer's lips as the gravity and double meaning of what I'd said registered.

"What I meant to say is do I look bad?"

I held my breath as Hammer surveyed me from head to toe, his gaze pausing as he studied my exposed legs.

Separating the distance between us, Hammer placed his finger under my chin, raising my face to his. "Sweetheart, you couldn't look bad if you tried." Wrapping his hand around my waist, "While you're rocking the fuck out of this dress, I won't lie, I liked what you said the first time."

Searching his deep eyes, I tried in vain to find any hint of a lie. When nothing but sincerity reflected back at me, I let my passion loose, pulling him down and pressing my lips to his.

"Make me forget," I begged as I drifted my fingers from his chest to the string of his shorts.

Hammer deepened the kiss, palming my face in his hands as he backed me into the wall.

"Forget what?" Dropping his lips to my neck, Hammer bent down, lifting me up, placing my center on his hips. He felt so heavy against me, so powerful.

"Later." Slipping my hand into the band of his shorts, I grazed my fingers over the head of his penis.

"This changes everything," Hammer stilled my hand. "I refuse to have a taste of you only for you to leave me in the end. I know I hurt you, and I'm sorry, but please, don't punish me like this."

Laying my head against the wall, I could feel the heaviness in the room. Standing at the proverbial crossroads, the decision for me was easy. With Clark everything was calculated, planned, with no room for growth. Hammer was everything I'd tried to convince myself I didn't want, yet silently craved.

"I don't want just a taste either."

Hammer's eyes danced between mine before he took a deep breath. "You better hold on, baby."

Hungry lips crashed to mine as the room around me swirled. Hammer's tongue swiped against my lips as he laid me down on what I assumed was his bed.

"You don't know how many times I've fantasized about you lying in my bed." His voice husky, dripping with desire as he laid kisses down my chest and shoulder. "How many dreams I've had of diving between your sweet thighs."

Sitting back on his thighs, his bulging erection attempting to break out of its cotton prison. "The motherfucker who told you this dress wasn't for you, knew he would never have the pleasure of seeing it crumpled on his bedroom floor." Laying his hands on my thighs, Hammer began pushing his way up, slipping his fingers under the hem I'd worked so hard to keep down. "The hateful shit he said to you, was in hopes you'd run home and cry into your pillow, instead of screaming into it like I'm planning for you to do."

A gasp left my lips as his fingers reached the band of my panties. I didn't own sexy lingerie and, until this moment, I'd never regretted it.

"I told you." A smile curled at the corner of Hammer's lips, his gaze moved to my panties as he tossed them over his shoulder. "Next time, I was tasting from the source."

A cry left my lips as my back arched in response to the feel of Hammer's mouth covering my slit. Grasping the comforter, my breath was lost to the feeling of his tongue lapping at my clit. Hammer gripped the back of my thighs, forcing them toward my center before taking a slow and deliberate lick. As he circled my clit, he dropped my left thigh, snaking his fingers into my entrance.

"Hammer," I chanted as a wave of euphoria began to build.

"That's it, baby, wear it out." Pulling my clit between his teeth and nibbling. "Make my neighbors jealous of what I'm doing to you."

My orgasm hit like a freight train, leaving me dazed and confused.

"Fuck, that was beautiful." I vaguely heard Hammer say before the feeling of his lips surrounding my nipple pulled me back to reality. Glancing down, I watched as Hammer's cheeks hollowed out as he sucked on the tender flesh. The sight of his tongue flicking the peak had me grinding my core against him.

"Patience, sweetheart, we'll get there." He winked as he switched breasts, his eyes locked with mine as he repeated his actions.

Crawling up my body, Hammer nipped my skin, soothing it with his tongue when I jumped from the pinch. When we were face to face, Hammer placed gentle kisses to my neck and cheek, something was reflecting in his eyes I couldn't quite decipher.

"What is it?" The insecurities gifted me came to the surface, causing my heart to race and panic to rise.

"You are so much more beautiful than in my dreams," Hammer moved a piece of my hair from my face, running his fingers along the edge of my chin as he studied my face. "You make me want things." Running his nose along mine before covering my lips with his own. I was on fire for this man, my body craving more of his touch.

"Are you on anything?" He questioned against my lips.

Shaking my head, embarrassment heating my cheeks and neck.

"What?" Hammer angled his head to the side in confusion.

"I, um," hesitating, I looked beyond him to the ceiling.

"Hey, it's just you and me." Placing a kiss to my cheek before reaching into the nightstand.

"It's not that," pointing to the foil wrapper poised between his teeth. Hammer remained silent, opening the package as he waited for me to continue.

"This is so stupid, but you have a right to know." Swallowing thickly, I concentrated on the sound of him sliding the latex over his erection.

"Growing up in the biker community, sex was something you either saw or heard almost every day. I'd heard the horror stories of a girl's first time and I didn't want the embarrassment of bleeding all over the guys junk and sheets when it finally happened. So, I bought a vibrator and broke my hymen myself."

Hammer nodded his head and he lined himself up to my entrance, running the head back and forth through my slick folds.

"So, you've never had a real cock inside your pussy?" He slipped the tip in slightly, a gasp leaving my lips at the sensation. "Broken hymen or not, you're a goddamn virgin." He'd smiled at the latter and pushed himself in further. "And you're fucking mine." He added through clenched teeth as he buried himself to the hilt.

My eyes squeezed shut at the sensation of him inside me. Broken hymen or not, he was so much bigger than the silicone dick I'd used.

"Emma?"

My eyes flashed open at the tremble in his voice.

"Are you okay? Do we need to stop?"

"No, I'm okay. Just didn't think it would hurt so—"

"I can fix that," he mumbled before flipping us over so I was hovering over him. "Make yourself feel good, babe. Tell me what you need."

Glancing down, I perused his muscled chest as I adjusted my legs. Placing my hands on his toned pecs, I lifted my pelvis and slowly sank back down. Hammer extended his thumb toward my face.

"Open," he commanded, gathering saliva on the digit before pressing it to my clit and circling. "Better?" He raised an eyebrow as my pelvis mimicked his rhythm.

Nodding my head, I kept my gaze on him. I watched as he dropped his eyes to his hand before returning them to my face. When he licked his lips and opened his mouth, my body acted of its own accord as I leaned over, placing a nipple on his waiting tongue. Something in me snapped as his lips closed around the sensitive flesh, my hips shifted from up and down to sliding against his pelvis. Hammer removed his thumb, as I tossed my head back.

"Yes," I moaned, picking up speed as the same tidal wave began to build.

"You look so good riding my cock." Sitting up, Hammer changed the angle of my clit hitting his pelvis. Wrapping his arms around me, he flipped us again, the movement causing the title wave to crash and his name to leave my lips.

Hammer took over, lifting my left leg and placing it between us as he pushed in and out of me. He was so incredible, so handsome, as he hovered over me.

Feeling brave, I reached up. "Open," I commanded, gathering his saliva on my index finger. Looking down, I watched the spot where we were joined, placing my wet finger on my clit as I kept time with him thrusting in and out of me.

"See that?" He panted.

"Yes," not bothering to look away as I sped up my fingers.

"You're mine, Emma Shaw," he swore as his thrusts increased. "All of you." He pulled back, sitting on his heels and gripping my hips he began pulling us together. "Your tight as fuck pussy, incredible tits, and that fucking sweet mouth of yours." Throwing his head back, his thrusts increased rapidly. "All motherfucking mine," he roared, pushing in and staying inside me.

I felt him swell, the sensation forcing a hiss from my lips as he hit something deep inside me, invoking a tiny wave to crash around me.

Hammer pulled out, dropping his body beside me, pulling me to his chest. "I didn't hurt you, did I?"

Laying my hand on his chest, I could feel his beating heart under my fingertips. "No."

Reaching down, he slipped his fingers under my chin, lifting my face toward his. "I meant what I said."

Confused, I pulled back, "Wh—"

Hammer silenced me by placing his lips against mine, sliding his knee between my thighs as pushed me into the mattress.

"You are mine, Emma Shaw," he whispered against my lips, spearing his fingers into the hair at the nape of my neck.

Searching my eyes, he ran the tip of his nose along mine as he placed a kiss to the edge of my lips. "I love you."

My eyes fluttered open, the pressure in my bladder the culprit for waking me. Pulling back the blanket, I moved to get out of bed when the tattooed arm held me back. Glancing over my shoulder, I came face to face with a still sleeping Hammer. As carefully as I could, I lifted his arm and slipped out of the bed. Not sure which door was the bathroom, I used the odds he would leave the bathroom door open as I slipped inside, closing the door before feeling for the switch on the wall.

Just as the living room shocked me, the master bathroom took my breath away. Granite and marble ran fluidly beside one another. A glass enclosed shower took up the far wall, its confines large enough for at least three people. Crossing the sizable space, I sat on the toilet, reaching to my left for the toilet paper. As I emptied my bladder, I scanned the room, taking in the modern details. Finishing up, I hesitated as I pushed the button on the toilet to flush. As I moved to leave, I caught sight of a bottle of feminine wash on the shelf in the shower.

"Kira," my heart sank as her name left my lips. With the events of the night, I'd forgotten about the woman who was as close to a wife as you could get without paperwork. Of course she would have things in his house, they'd lived as a family until recently. Approaching the sink, I caught my reflection as I twisted the faucet and ran my hands under the cold water.

"She's Liam's mother," I spoke to the woman in the mirror. "And a permanent part of his life." Dropping my gaze, I shut off the water, drying my hands on one of the pristine towels hanging beside the sink. "But he loves you," I reminded her before reaching for the switch and stepping from the room.

Hammer was in the same position as I'd left him. He'd woken me twice in the night, exploring new positions each time. Kneeling at the foot of the bed, I licked my lips at the memory of the way he'd wrapped his body around mine, slipping his cock inside me from behind as he played with my clit until I'd screamed his name.

With a fire igniting in my core, I crawled up the bed, pulling back the covers to reveal his naked body. Combing my hair to the side, I leaned over and poked my tongue out, licking the head of his soft cock. When Hammer failed to respond, I did it again, this time using my hand to lift him as I took most of him in my mouth.

"Hmm," his throaty reply severed the silence in the room.

Encouraged, I began pumping my hand up and down his shaft, swirling my tongue around the head. One minute he's flaccid as a piece of overcooked spaghetti, and the next, he's stiff as a board, and his fingers were sliding into the back of my bobbing head.

"Fuck, baby," Hammer swore as he turned on his back, the bedside table light snapping on, causing me to flinch from the bright intrusion. "Sorry, but I have to see you sucking my cock."

Smiling, I wrapped my hand around his shaft, giving him several pumps before lowering my mouth and circling his head with my tongue.

"Motherfucker," he swore as he ran his thumb along my lip. A hiss left his lips as I accidentally scraped the underside with my teeth. "Do that shit again, baby."

His request surprised me, however I did as he asked and gently placed my bottom teeth on him again. Hammer slammed his head against the wood of the headboard, his fingers digging into my hair as he began thrusting his hips.

"Too fucking close," he muttered a split second before he pulled me off, replacing his cock with his tongue as he laid me across the bed on my stomach. Jumping from the bed, Hammer moved between my dangling legs as he lifted my hips off the bed and plunged into me from behind.

"I love taking you like this," he confessed into my ear as he laid his front over my back, his hand kneading my left breast. "Your pussy fits me like a fucking glove. And your ass," he pulled away, running a finger around my puckered hole. "Fuck baby, I want to fill this one day."

The building orgasm inside of me tapped down my fear of anal sex, while the sensation of his circling finger sent me spiraling over the edge.

Hammer collapsed on the bed beside me, his labored breathing making me smile. Turning on my side to face him, I couldn't contain the smile on my face as I took him in. I, Emma Shaw, extreme conservative, had made bad ass biker Hammer Sheppard, sweat and swear during sex.

"I love you," Hammer lifted a finger, drifting it along my chin.

Taking his hand in mine, I brought it to my lips, placing a kiss to his knuckles. Lifting my gaze to his, "I love you too."

Hammer

CHAPTER
TWENTY-EIGHT
HAMMER

"SO, tell me how you got the road name Hammer?" Emma stood cooking breakfast in one of my SOC T-shirts, her beautiful legs driving me crazy as I watched her move around my kitchen.

"Awe, babe, don't make me tell you that. I just got you and it doesn't leave me in a good light."

Spinning on her heels, the hem of my shirt flared out giving me a glimpse of her naked cheeks. "You forget, I lived with a man who believed, and I quote, 'pussy is pussy, as long as you're getting it, doesn't matter where it came from'."

Standing to my full height, I made my way around the bar. Despite Emma's understanding of the twisted thoughts of an outlaw biker, I would need to do some damage control with this one. "About a year after I became a prospect, my father, along with Farrah's dad, who was the president at the time, threw this huge ass party. At the time, SOC and Disciples were practically the same, so they invited all these girls."

I inwardly cringed as Emma laid down the spatula in her hand and crossed her arms over her chest. The raised eyebrow over her left eye gave away the growing jealousy inside her.

"I was all of nineteen and perpetually horny. So, when a group of those girls invited me to join them." I shrugged, intentionally leaving out the part where we didn't bother to find somewhere private. The four of them had stripped naked, laying with their asses up along the bar.

"Farrah's dad came in as I was..." I trailed off, unable to look at Emma.

"Fucking?" She finished for me, the curse coming from her lips making my dick twitch to life. Approaching Emma like a lion trying to mate with his lioness, I grabbed her arm and pulled her to me.

"Yes, baby, fucking." Leaning down, I nibbled at her bottom lip as I backed her against the counter of my center island. "He'd said something about hammering it home and the name stuck."

Emma squealed as I placed her on the counter, lifting the hem of my shirt and spreading her legs wide as I dove between her legs. I'd eaten a lot of pussy in my life, but none tasted as good as Emma's.

"Hammer," she called as I ran my flattened tongue along her slit.

I'd learned from the handful of times I'd been between her thighs, what she did and didn't like me to do. I planned to show her so many things, find out what made her happy and what got my face slapped.

"Lay back, baby."

Placing my hand on the center of her stomach, I gently nudged her where I wanted her, with her knees spread and pussy begging for my touch. I eased my fingers into her, curling them as I searched for the spot which made her scream. Joining my fingers with my tongue, I lapped at her clit, alternating between suction and gentle nips of my teeth. It had made my fucking day to learn Emma liked a little pain with her pleasure, much as I did. When her legs began shaking, I knew she was close. Quickening my movements, I raised my gaze to find Emma propped on her elbows, her eyes locked on mine. Keeping my fingers inside of her, I moved to within inches of her face, my eyes dancing between hers.

"I told you to lay back."

"You did." Her breath washed over my face, the sweet smell of her making me impossibly harder. "But as of yesterday, I no longer work for you."

Confused, I cocked my head to the side.

"Besides," Emma moved her face closer to mine, sticking out her tongue and swiping it along my bottom lip. "I like watching your tongue lick my pussy."

Sucking her tongue into my mouth, I stilled my fingers inside her, eliciting a disappointed moan. Ending the kiss, "Want my tongue in your pussy?" Pulling my fingers out, I brought them to her mouth, coating her swollen lips with her juices.

"Yes," she admitted, her tongue poking out and licking her lips.

Pushing my shorts to the floor, I hopped on the counter beside her. Laying on my back, I tapped my chin, "Hop on, baby."

Emma looked at me, confusion coloring her beautiful face. Reaching over, I gripped her hand, pulling her toward me. Her mouth dropped open as she realized what I had in mind. Laying my head back down, I opened my mouth as Emma straddled my face, lowering her pussy onto my wagging tongue.

"Shit," she exclaimed as I felt her hands fall onto my chest.

Reaching down, I pinched one of her nipples before lowering my hand and stroking my hard cock. Emma picked up speed as she rode my tongue, a near silent oath left her lips a second before I felt her warm hand cover mine as she swallowed the head of my cock. Once again, I let her get her fill, grinding her sweet pussy on my face as she rode her way to an orgasm. I couldn't recall a time when I'd held my cock while a girl sucked me off, but as Emma's wet lips connected with my fingers, my balls grew tighter. Knowing I wasn't going to last much longer, I used my free hand to kneed her tit as I caught her clit and sucked. Her orgasm followed mine as I held her tight so she could enjoy the aftershocks.

"I need a favor," Emma smiled as she dried her hair with a towel.

"Babe, I'm going to need at least an hour before we go again." Wrapping my body around her, I nipped at her shoulder.

"I need a ride to get my car."

Locking eyes with her in the mirror, "Of course. Besides, there's something I need to grab for you at the Club anyway."

"My car is at—"

"You're not driving that piece of shit anymore, Emma."

I could see in her eyes she wanted to argue. However, since Emma was the daughter of chapter president, she knew what being with me entailed.

"The Mercedes is gassed and ready unless you'd like something else."

"What I'd like," Emma's hands stilled as she moved her gaze to the shower. "Is not to have to look at Kira's things if this is going to be a regular thing."

Following her line of sight, I saw the purple bottle sitting on the shelf. Clearing the distance, I picked up the offending item. "This?" I held it up.

"Yes. I'd rather not have the reminder that she has a vagina she cleaned while I'm in there with you."

Tossing the bottle into the trash. "First of all, this is most definitely going to be a regular thing," I pointed between us. "Second, the bottle wasn't Kira's. Liam tossed it into my shopping cart one day and insisted he wanted to use the pretty soap. I honestly forgot about it until now." Spinning her around to face me. "You never have to worry about Kira ever again."

Emma dropped her eyes to my chin, "She's Liam's mom. She will always—"

"The judge ruled in my favor yesterday," I cut her off, caging her in my arms. "Based on all the evidence Hailey presented, Kira was stripped of her parental rights."

Emma searched my face before wrapping her arms around my neck. "I'm so sorry, Hammer," she whispered into my ear. "That had to be so difficult for you." Placing a kiss to my cheek, she pulled away, running her thumbs along the side of my jaw.

"When Liam was born, my father told me there would be times when I had to do things in his best interests I didn't necessarily want to do. Never, in my wildest dreams, did I think it would be to sever ties with the woman who gave birth to him."

Emma

CHAPTER
TWENTY-NINE
EMMA

THE CLUBHOUSE WAS a flurry of activity as Hammer pulled us into the lot. Warden stood beside Daxx, a smile on their faces and beers in hand. Erin and Jillian sat atop a wooden picnic table as the grill behind them billowed with smoke.

"What's going on?"

"I forgot to tell you," holding out his hand for me, Hammer looked at me over his shoulder. "Syn had her baby."

Hammer's explanation was a harsh reminder I no longer had a job with SOC. While the money I'd earned from representing Warden was enough to carry me over, I worried about taking care of Jackson without having a job.

"Come on, let's get something to eat. Someone let breakfast burn and refused to make any more."

"Hey, I'm not the one who felt the need to have a shower instead of making food." I reminded him, the memory of him tossing me over his shoulder and running down the hall to his ensuite. He'd sat me on the bench, washing my entire body before pinning me to the glass and getting me dirty again.

"Totally worth the risk of starvation," he wiggled his eyebrows before laying a scorching kiss to my lips.

"Emma, Emma, Emma." Daxx called my name as he and Warden crossed the parking lot toward us. "Who'd have guessed there was such fire hiding underneath all of that—"

"Finish that fucking sentence and I'll cut your tongue off." Hammer placed his body between mine and Daxx's. "As much as Emma was off limits before, she's untouchable now."

My breath hitched inside my throat. Property patching was one thing, but calling me untouchable was on an entirely different level.

"Are you serious, bro?" Daxx opened his arms wide, taking Hammer into a side hug. "Better you than me."

"I want to thank you again, for yesterday," Warden laid a hand on my elbow. "Daxx is right, I never would have guessed you possessed so much fire in your belly. I wouldn't be surprised if Boom was still scratching his head as to what happened."

Scanning the lot, I looked for Hailey but came up empty. I'd given my word not to say anything and I didn't want to accidentally break a promise.

"Hey, just because I don't care for Ace, doesn't mean I didn't pay attention when he talked." I'd learned from Ace how to zero in on someone's weaknesses and capitalize on them. I'd watched how he'd twist words to confuse the speaker, giving him time to obtain the element of surprise.

"I'm just glad things didn't get physical. I haven't brought a man to his knees since my first year in college."

Hammer wrapped himself around me, burying his nose in the crook of my neck. "You had me on my knees twice last night."

Turning my head to kiss him, the sound of heavy metal music and the roar of an engine pulled my attention to the gate. Farrah's white convertible sped through the entrance, Kira standing in the passenger seat, pointing in our direction.

"Where is my fucking kid, asshole?" She demanded, jumping from the car and almost tripping in her ridiculously high heels.

Hammer stepped around me. "Would you look at that? You are alive. What's wrong, Ray grow tired of tying a board across his ass so he wouldn't fall in?"

A warm hand engulfed mine. Looking to my left, I saw Erin's worried face staring at mine.

"He doesn't have to. His cock is big enough, unlike your pencil dick."

An involuntary snort came out of my nose, capturing Kira's attention. Despite my lack of real sexual partners, the ache between my thighs completely contradicted her witty comeback.

"Oh my god," Farrah threw her head back in laughter. "You can put away those delusions of happily ever after dancing in your eyes. You fucked him, after everything I told you."

"Farrah," Warden warned, motioning for her to join him. "This doesn't concern you."

"It's fine, sis." Kira waved off Farrah, hooking her hands on her hips and turning back to Hammer. "He can have all the side action he wants. We both know he'll never replace me." The brow over her left eye raised in what I suspected was an invitation to challenge.

"You're right, Kira, I did try to replace you over the last five years. Trouble was," Hammer stopped, a huff leaving his throat as he looked down at me. "I didn't feel any attachment to any of them." Sending me a wink, Hammer turned back to Kira. "Which is why I let you back in, over and over again."

Hammer reached back, taking my hand in his, "Not this time, Kira. I'm over being comfortable with you. I'm in love with Emma, something I never felt for you."

My heart broke for Kira as I watched the light dim in her eyes in reaction to Hammer's confession. Had she truly loved him? Or was she grieving for something else?

"Fine, you can keep your whore, but I'm taking my son. Hurry up, I have shit to do." As quickly as the sadness appeared in her eyes, it was replaced with the fury I'd come to expect from her.

"Well, had you bothered to show up for court yesterday, you would know the judge terminated your rights."

I expected Kira to break off into a tirade, scream and hit Hammer until he restrained her. However, nothing could have prepared me for the callus words which left her mouth.

"Whatever, Hammer, keep your stupid brat. Ray can give me all the kids I want."

Rage filled my body as Liam's sweet face filled my mind. "How fucking dare you?" I growled because all I could see was red. Dropping Erin's hand, I stepped around Hammer, drawing my right fist back and letting it fly. I didn't feel any pain when my fist connected with Kira's face, nor did I have any inkling to stop when I saw the blood dripping down her face. One minute I was being supportive of Hammer and the next I was straddling Kira, throwing punch after punch at her face and body.

"Babe," I could hear Hammer's voice, but my rage was still flowing, fueling each strike. "Emma, stop." I heard him roar as an arm wrapped around my middle, pulling me high into the air.

"You broke my nose, you stupid bitch." I heard Kira scream as Hammer placed me back on the ground. "You're dead. I don't give a shit who your daddy is, I'm going to fucking end you." She continued to roar as my hands began to shake from the release of adrenaline.

"Look at me," Hammer demanded, his hands gripping my shoulders. "Are you okay?" His pleading eyes nearly broke me.

"I'm fine," I managed, holding up my right hand which had several smears of bright crimson on it. "I may need a tetanus shot."

Motion from behind Hammer caught both of our attention. Two police cars pulled into the lot followed by a black sedan. My heart hovered in my throat as two uniformed officers emerged from their vehicles and began walking toward us. I'd never been arrested, and as I looked at the pair, I could see my new job fading from my grasp.

"Warden," The first officer greeted, extending his hand out to shake.

"Hey, man, what's going on?"

"Afraid we are here on official business."

Warden crossed his arms over his chest, "Sounds serious."

"Kira Rogers?" A man in a suit called, his badge held high over his head as he walked around the officers. "You're under arrest for the murder of officer Raymond Johnson."

My hand covered my mouth in shock as the officer placed Kira in handcuffs.

"You're making a mistake. Hammer, do something," she demanded as they escorted her to the closest police car. Hammer remained silent as they placed her inside the car and closed the door.

Warden spoke with the man in the suit for several minutes as Kira screamed and pounded her head on the window. With a quick hand-shake, the three climbed back into their cars.

"Meeting in five minutes," Warden barked as the police cars pulled into traffic.

"Make it ten, Warden. There's something I need to do." Lacing his fingers with mine, Hammer led me into the Clubhouse, passed the kitchen and through the door I knew housed the private quarters of the brothers.

"You can use the bathroom to clean up." Stepping over the threshold, my mouth agape as I took in the room. Unlike his home, the room was stark and lacked any personal touches.

"What is this?"

"Now, I know Ace has quarters like this. I stayed in one of them a few years ago."

Nodding, "Oh, he does, but I'm used to them resembling a fraternity house and not an office."

Hammer turned his back toward me as he walked to the corner of the room. "It used to." Bending at the knees, he moved a stack of boxes to reveal a safe on the wall. "When Keys patched in, I let him have my furniture."

Something told me there was more to the story, but like most things in a biker's world I wasn't privy to the information.

"I'm going to clean up," pointing to the door to my left, I slipped inside before Hammer could say anything.

Closing the door, I wasted zero time as I approached the sink, twisting on the tap and began scrubbing the blood from my hands. Sending a silent prayer of thanks when the final swirl of red disappeared down the drain, my hands free from any cuts.

Drying my hands, I twisted open the door, finding Hammer sitting on the floor, an envelope dangling between his bent legs.

"Come sit," he patted the floor. "I have something to show you."

Tossing the towel into the sink, I crossed the room and dropped to the floor in front of him.

"I know you have an aversion to the whole property patch thing." Tossing the black square into the space between us, his road name scrolled in orange against the dark background. "You're in good company with your beliefs, as both Erin and Jillian took issue with it too."

"Is that why you said I'm untouchable?"

Shaking his head, Hammer grimaced. "I did it, because you mean so much more to me than what that patch conveys."

Reaching out, Hammer picked up the envelope, twirling it around in his fingers.

"Emma, I want to share so many things with you; my home, my heart, my last name. Eventually," he added, making me smile. "Please," his voice cracked. "Don't take the job with the IRS. Stay here at SOC, stay with me."

"I—"

"I worked it all out," he interrupted, ripping open the envelope and unfolding the page inside. "You'll have all of our accounts, plus Kumarin's and a few of his associates are interested in talking with you. The building is in your name. All you have to do is tell Keys what equipment you want and he will make it happen."

With shaky fingers, I reached out and took the letter.

"It's in the same strip mall as Jillian's shop. You can take on private clients, and hire whomever you want. Just, please, don't leave."

I opened and closed my mouth several times as I tried to take it all in. "Hammer, Jillian's shop is inside some prime real estate. Are you sure about this? I mean you could make a fortune in rent."

Scooting closer to me, Hammer palmed my face, "I don't need another fortune, I need you."

Searching his face, I reached out, tracing my fingers along his jaw.

"Yes," I whispered, my throat clogged with emotion. "Yes to the job, the house, and especially your heart. And eventually, yes to your last name."

Hammer

EPILOGUE
HAMMER

"THOMPSON SAID they found Ray out by the railroad tracks not far from the bath house."

I half listened to Warden, choosing instead to keep my attention on Kumarin as he spoke with Emma.

"Do you really think Kira has the ability to kill someone?"

Doc Ash and Drew brought Liam and Jackson over after an excited Emma told Erin she was staying in Detroit.

"She allegedly killed the guys who'd kidnapped her in Russia," I thought out loud. "Maybe she got tired of telling him no, like the guys who dragged her to America. Or maybe, he was the one who attacked her outside of Distractions."

A pang of jealousy slammed into me as I watched Emma hug Kumarin. I reminded myself he was stupidly in love with his wife, Natalia. So much so, he was begging her to have more babies with him.

"I don't think she did," Daxx added. "I clearly heard her say, Ray could give her as many kids as she wanted."

The room fell silent as many heads nodded in agreement.

"Say the word Hammer and I'll put Kannon on her case."

Shifting my attention to Warden, "Not just no, but hell no. Kira is no longer under the protection of this club and has no interests in any of its members. What I do want to get to the bottom of is who took the guns bound for Kumarin? Why didn't Boom mention Hailey to Emma when he was listing his demands? And who the fuck is this Frank guy?"

Daxx cleared his throat, "I was able to zoom in on the tattoo on his forearm. I showed it to our friend Einstein who said it looked like the Cavanagh family crest, but there wasn't enough showing for confirmation."

Warden found Einstein on the Dark Web, he'd worked with an organization called Keystone who specialized in extractions and killings for hire.

"Why would the Cavanagh's get involved with a two-bit asshole like Boom?"

Warden's question weighed heavily in the room.

"I'm not sure, but I suspect we're about to find out."

Standing to my full height, "Gentlemen, we have a party going on outside and some insanely beautiful women who deserve our attention."

Bullet jumped to his feet, "And I have a fiancée who has wedding shit to show me."

Jillian and Bullet decided to have the wedding in the park where they met, and the reception at his bar where he'd first confessed his love for her.

"And I need to get something from you to give to Emma." I pointed to Daxx.

Our boots echoed as Daxx and I made our way to his room. He'd commandeered the room at the end of the hall as it had a door leading to the alley.

"You sure about this?" Daxx questioned as he spun the lock on his safe.

"As sure as the day I slipped this Cut on for the first time."

Closing the door and spinning the lock. "Better you than me, brother. Too many fine women in the world to settle for one."

"Your day will come, Daxx. Love will bite you in the ass when you least expect it."

"Have you met me? I'm the poster child for all things man whore."

"True," I shrugged, pocketing the box in my front pocket. "However, the right woman can make all the difference."

As we turned to head to the party, Daxx stopped abruptly twisting his head to the side. "Do you hear that?"

"What?" I began, but Daxx was headed out the door and toward the back of the club.

"That," he exclaimed as we rounded the building.

Listening hard, I heard the faint sounds of what sounded like a symphony.

"What the fuck?" Daxx took several measured steps before bending over and picking up an extension cord. Without a word, Daxx followed the cord, hand over hand until it disappeared through a slit in the fence. Dropping the cord, Daxx jumped up, gripped the top of the fencepost and lifted himself up.

"What the...?" He drifted off, his eyes squinting as he stared at the building beyond the fence. SOC owned the majority of the property on this street, the building behind us being a two-story storage facility.

"Well, well, well, would you look who I found."

CHAPTER 30
SAMPLE FROM BOOK FOUR: DAXX

CHAPTER One

Milania

I held my breath as I kept my back to the metal wall, the muscles of my toes burning as I balanced on the ledge. I considered tossing my backpack to the ground but worried the collision would break something or the men searching for me would hear it.

"I'm telling you, Hammer, I saw Milania standing right here."

Squeezing my eyes shut as my name found my ears, I sent up a silent prayer the men on the other side of this wall would give up searching for me before the muscles in my legs did. This had been a mistake. I knew I shouldn't have returned after the first time my electric cord was discovered.

"Well, she's gone now, Daxx," a second man laughed. "Come on, I need to go find Emma."

A part of me wished I could see their faces, know who they were and how they knew who I was. An even bigger part of me knew the answer, and silently damned the man who'd put me in this position.

"Hey, man, I believe you, but look around. She's long gone."

I waited for what felt like forever until I heard the sound of boots hitting the pavement. Releasing the breath I'd held, I counted to fifty before moving to the railing and climbing over.

Ignoring the pain in my feet, I ran as fast as I could down the alley and around the corner, not stopping until I reached the end of the street. Tossing my bag to the ground, I fell hard against the trunk of a massive tree, its girth more than enough to shield me from anyone passing by.

Reaching into my bag, I took out my tennis shoes, their material having seen better days. How long had it been since I'd purchased something new? Six months? Eight? Hell, I wasn't certain what month it was anymore.

I was so tired of running, surviving each day in fear of the next. In the blink of an eye, I'd gone from living a luxurious life to hustling for every penny I could find. From sleeping on thousand count thread sheets to finding a dry piece of hard ground. Winter had been the worst. With no coat, nor the ability to buy one, every bone in my body had ached until spring came.

Dancing was, and will always be, the one thing I used to escape the pitfalls of my life. I began dancing at the insistence of my mother. I could recall, standing in my first class at five years old, begging her to let me go home. She'd stood firm, encouraged me if I stayed for the hour, she'd let me decide whether I came back.

"I miss you, mom," whispering to the heavens as I slipped my throbbing feet into my shoes and stood to my full height. Glancing at my watch, a pang of guilt hit me as I read the time through the cracked glass. I'd traded the watch I was gifted at graduation for a ride to Detroit, a place where I'd foolishly assumed I could disappear, creating a new life.

Grabbing the straps of my backpack, I toss it over my shoulder before taking off down the alley toward the gym I'd been dropped off at when I first arrived. The building was nothing special, the facility used mostly by men who were training for underground fighting and a few women who found the manager attractive. If I hurried, I could get into the hot tub before his shift started.

Standing outside the gym, I scanned the area around me before inserting the key I'd found at work. Chandler, the night manager, had a habit of sliding keys to women he wanted to hook up with. When he offered one to a coworker, she'd waited long enough for him to leave before tossing it in the trash and telling the rest of us how big of a douchebag he was. Curiosity got the better of me, so I fished it out of the trash and ventured out to see if the key was legit.

Tossing my backpack into a locker, I stripped out of my yoga pants and leotard, wrapping a towel around my body as I toed off my tennis shoes. My narrow escape from earlier left the skin of my feet with a number of cuts, but nothing serious.

Padding through the door, the smell of chlorine burns my nose. Unlike the modern gyms down the street, this one is what my friend Veronica would label as vintage, with its stark white appearance and lack of any aesthetics. I find the hot tub blissfully empty, dropping my towel to the side, I take a tentative step into the steaming hot water, the chlorine burning the cuts in my feet, although not enough to deter me. Sinking into the bubbling water, I make my way to the furthest corner, closing my eyes and dreaming of the day I have enough money to move across the border to Canada.

After tonight, I know my time in Detroit is limited. I needed a new identity, but buying one of those is expensive. I've managed to tuck away more than half of what I need, and hope like hell I can hide out long enough to earn the rest. I've heard rumors that Gulio placed a bounty over my head. Granted, he labeled it a reward, however I knew the truth. A life as his wife would be the third level of hell.

The sound of the door closing forces my eyes open. Glancing at the end of the pool, I see a couple enter the room. Reaching for the towel behind me, I hide my face as I pretend not to notice them. The woman is beautiful, her dark hair pulled up at the top of her head, a sparkly bikini adorning her sculpted body. She has a tattoo on her neck, a name I think, but she's too far away to be sure. My breath catches as I take in the familiar features of the man, my heart pounding as I turn my back toward them, trying to become invisible.

"It's been so long since I've had you alone."

I heard the man groan, his deep voice making me nauseous. I thought of the last time I saw him, a few summers ago when I'd stopped in to visit my father at his office. He'd flirted, told me all the things he could do for me, as long as I gave him what he wanted.

"You have no idea how much I've missed this," the woman purred. "Hammer and his bullshit has made my life a living hell."

My eyes grew wide as I heard her say the name of one of the guys from earlier

"I know, sweetheart. It won't be much longer until Warden and his band of misfits get what's coming to them."

Despite the heat of the water, a chill ran down my spine as I took in the conversation. Knowing the character of the man, I have no doubt he intends to harm this Warden.

"You've said that before, yet here I am."

"Hey, you know what happened with Boom wasn't my fault."

"Then who's to blame? Weren't you the one who hand picked these men?"

"Listen, sweetheart, you keep playing your role and leave this to me. I promise, this will all be over soon and you and I—"

"Don't say it. Actions, my love, not words." The woman chastised. "Now, let's get out of here, my skin is pruning and you promised me a night I would remember."

I remained perfectly still until I was certain the couple was gone. Springing from the water, I wrapped the towel around my body and ran into the locker room. I didn't know who the woman was, but I didnt want to stick around long enough to find out.

Throwing my clothes on, I reached for my bag, but my nerves got the best of me and I dropped the bag, the contents spilling to the carpeted floor. Bending down, I pick up my ballet shoes, winding the ribbons around and shoving them into my bag. I saw one of my silicone pads, but as I searched my bag, I couldn't find the other.

"Dang it," I huffed, sitting back on my heels as I weighed my options. I could dance without them, however I'd learned the hard way my feet paid the ultimate price when I did. There wasn't an athletic shop anywhere close and buying online wasn't an option as I didn't have a credit card. My only choice was to retrace my steps.

Shoving the lone pad into my bag, I checked to see if the coast was clear before stepping into the hallway. Shouldering my bag, I was nearly to the exit when I saw Chandler coming out of his office. Ducking my head, I walked with purpose, hoping he wouldn't notice me as he'd been looking at his cellphone. With my hand on the handle of the door, I was about to breathe a sigh of relief when I heard his voice.

"Hey, don't I know you?"

CODE OF SILENCE SERIES

THE BAD BOYS OF THE MAFIA.

Shamrocks & Secrets

Claddagh & Chaos

Stolen Secrets

Secret Sin

Secret Atonement

Family Secrets

Buried Secrets

Secrets & Lies Coming soon

SOUTHERN JUSTICE TRILOGY
WHEN THE GOOD GUYS FOLLOW THE BAD BOY'S RULES.

Absolute Power

Absolute Corruption

Absolute Valor

TRIDENT BROTHERHOOD SERIES
HOT SEALS. NEED I SAY MORE?

Signed, SEALed, Delivered

Operation SEAL

SEAL's Regret

SEAL the Deal

SEAL's Heart

SEAL's Honor

Walking the Bird.

HOSTILE TAKEOVER
A BILLIONAIRE ROMANCE

Hostile Takeover

ANGEL KISS
A PARANORMAL ROMANCE

Angel Kiss

JUSTICE

REVENGE REALLY IS BEST SERVED...

Justice

CRAIN'S LANDING
A STICKY SWEET ROMANCE

Crain's Landing

ABOUT THE AUTHOR

Cayce Poponea is a USA Today bestselling author. A true romantic at heart, she writes the type of fiction she loves to read. With strong female characters who are not easily swayed by the devilishly good looks and charisma of the male leads. All served with a twist you may never see coming. While Cayce believes falling in love is a hearts desire, she also feels men should capture our souls as well as turn our heads.

From the Mafia men who take charge, to the military men who are there to save the damsel in distress, her characters capture your heart and imagination. She encourages you to place your real life on hold and escape to a world where the laundry is all done, the bills are all paid and the men are a perfect as you allow them to be.

Cayce lives her own love story in Georgia with her husband, and three dogs. Leave your cares behind and settle in with the stories she creates just for you.

Made in the USA
Columbia, SC
23 April 2024